A Good Head on his Shoulders

(*La Tête sur les Epaules*)

Henri Troyat

Translated from the French, with a résumé of the author's
life and brief explanatory notes on the text, by Roy Ludlow

ELSP

Published in 2021
and reprinted in 2022
by ELSP
www.ex-librisbooks.co.uk

Origination by Ex Libris Press
Bradford on Avon, Wiltshire

Typeset in 10/13 point Chaparral Pro

Printed by CPC Ltd., Malmesbury

ISBN 978-1-912020-50-8

All enquiries and correspondence regarding this
book should be addressed to the translator at
royludlowd4@gmail.com

CONTENTS

Foreword   5

Author and translator   7

A GOOD HEAD ON HIS SHOULDERS   9

Notes   145

FOREWORD

My first encounter with this wonderful novel was some forty years ago, when I taught it as an A-Level French set text. I immediately fell in love with it. And what an inspired choice by the examination board! Here was a fairly short work, beautifully written in accessible French, telling a compelling story, the main character of which was a young man of eighteen, barely older than my students, and so someone with whom they could readily identify. Add to this, the fact that the young man was an intriguing character, caught up in difficult and fascinating circumstances, and we could not go wrong.

At about the same time I taught another fine novel by the same author, *La Neige en Deuil*, translated into English as *The Mountain*. After this, I was well and truly hooked on Henri Troyat. Over the years his novels have never failed to give me much pleasure.

I have never been able to track down a translation of *La Tête sur les Epaules*, even in recent times with an online search. (This does not mean that one does not exist, of course.) I have often felt that I would like to undertake the task myself, but it remained no more than an idea – until the lockdowns of the past year, that is. Paradoxically, circumstances which have curtailed so many opportunities prompted me to seize this one.

As noted above, the French is fairly straightforward and does not present insuperable difficulties for the translator. I am saving Marcel Proust for later.

It is not necessary to read the notes in order to enjoy the novel. However, I would particularly refer readers to Note 1 on Chapter Eight. This helps elucidate the philosophical themes of the book.

A word on punctuation: I have followed the practice in the French text of introducing speech with one inverted comma, but not closing it with any punctuation. I think one quickly gets accustomed to this.

My sincere wish is that those who read this novel, in whichever language, will find in it the same pleasure and, indeed, joy, which I have done.

My grateful thanks are due to my wife, Kathryn, for reading, and correcting, the proofs; to my good friend, Revd. Antony Claridge, for suggesting the English title; and to my publisher, Roger Jones, who has been most helpful and a constant source of encouragement.

Roy Ludlow
Winsley
May 2021

Author and translator

Henri Troyat was born Lev Aslanovich Tarassov in Moscow in 1911. His family was very wealthy, his father having made a fortune in investments in railways and banking, and so his early childhood was a highly privileged one. There were several servants, among them a Swiss governess, of whom more in the next paragraph. At the time of the 1917 Revolution the family retreated to their vast estate in the Caucasus to await the outcome. When it became obvious that the Bolsheviks would take power, they escaped their native land by means of the last émigré boat to leave the Crimea. After a circuitous journey, via Constantinople (as it still was) and Venice, they arrived, and settled, in Paris. They adopted French names.

Sadly. the family experienced the classic problems of Russian exiles: loss of status, isolation and financial difficulties. Troyat drew on these themes in some of his later fiction. He himself, however, adapted well to life in the French capital. The language was no problem because he had been taught it by the Swiss governess. He attended the Lycée Pasteur and, later, studied Law at the Sorbonne. He acquired French citizenship in 1933 and was appointed as a civil servant, a post he held until 1942.

During this time he began his literary career and was soon very successful. In 1935 he won the Prix du Roman Populiste with his novel *Faux Jour* (*Deceptive Light*). There followed several novels in quick succession, one of which, *L'Araigne*, won the prestigious Prix Goncourt in 1938. Thus, by the age of 27, Troyat was relatively well known and prosperous.

After the Second World War, whilst continuing to write stand alone novels, such as *La Tête sur les Epaules*, published in 1951, he embarked on two innovations which would dominate his later work: the long novel cycle and biography. Some of the novel cycles were set in pre-revolutionary Russia, some in France, whilst others moved between the two. Some of the biographies were of leading figures in French literature, such as Balzac, Flaubert and Zola, while others dealt with similarly great Russian authors, for example, Dostoevsky, Tolstoy and Pushkin. Yet more were of Russian leaders: Catherine the Great, Peter the Great, Alexander I and Ivan the Terrible.

Henri Troyat was an extraordinarily prolific author, writing over sixty novels and, indeed, 105 books in all. Being considered a populist writer, his work was not highly regarded within fashionable French literary and intellectual circles. One cannot imagine that he lost too much sleep over that. Indeed, he was one of the most popular authors with French readers. In 1959, at the age of 47, he was elected to the Académie Française and, at the time of his death, was its oldest member. Maurice Druon, a fellow member said of him: 'He wrote a simple and clear language, a language that lasts, eternal French.'

Henri Troyat died at the great age of 95 on 4th March 2007. His funeral took place in the Russian Orthodox Cathedral of Saint-Alexandre Nevski in Paris.

He was married twice. His first marriage, to Miss Lisette Muller in 1939, ended in divorce. This marriage produced a son, Jean-Daniel. In 1948 he married a widow, Marguerite Saintagne, described as the love of his life. She died before him. From this marriage he had a stepdaughter, Michèle Troyat McKeown. He also had three grandchildren; and six great-grandchildren.

R.L.

Roy Ludlow grew up in Leyton, east London, in the 1950s and was educated at Sir George Monoux Grammar School, in the neighbouring borough of Walthamstow, and at Leeds University. From there he obtained an upper second class honours degree in French in 1967 and a PGCE the next year. There followed a career in secondary education spanning 37 years and culminating in the post of Headmaster of Beechen Cliff School, Bath, a position he held from 1990 until his retirement in 2005. This is his first foray into serious translation.
He lives with his wife Kathryn in a village in Wiltshire.

A Good Head on his Shoulders

Chapter One

'Go on, admit it, you're in love with him.

She shrugged her shoulders and carried on applying her make-up in front of the mirror. Sitting on the edge of the bath, his elbows on his knees, his back hunched, Etienne Martin closely observed his mother's every gesture.

'It doesn't bother me that you are in love with him. Actually, I'm pleased.

He waited for an expression of thanks, for a smile. The lipstick glided over her lips. Her whole face lit up around her neat and glowing mouth.

'You've changed your lipstick?

'The other was too mauve. It made my mouth look sad.

'Possibly...I thought it was fine...

From his earliest childhood, Etienne had enjoyed watching his mother putting on her make-up. Once again, he admired her small face with its well defined eye brows, its wide, dark eyes, its strong chin. Her pure, rather harsh features, a little faded, sat oddly with her slender, girlish figure. A blue dress, pleated at the bodice and with a white schoolgirl collar, emphasised further this impression of lingering youth and of fragility.

'If I were M Maxime Joubert, I would invite you to stay for dinner, said Etienne.

She laughed aloud, shaking her short hair:

'M Maxime Joubert has many other things to worry about. We are meeting to talk business...

'And he sends you flowers!

'Because he's a gentleman.

'Because he finds you attractive.

'You're stupid, Etienne! You must not...

He jumped up, took his mother's hands and, turning towards her, forcibly, looked her fiercely in the eye:

'Why are you secretive with me? I am not a child. At eighteen I believe

I have the right to know what exactly your intentions are for the future. I could advise you, help you....must you really go to Lyon?

'Yes, I must, Etienne. M Joubert has been kind enough to give me an introduction to the Alfar Textile Company. If they agree to work with me, then I shall make clothes in bulk. It will be excellent business; I should make a fortune...

'When are you leaving?

'Probably the day after tomorrow. M Joubert will tell me this evening when exactly the meeting he has arranged will take place.

'He will go with you, of course!

She blushed:

'Certainly not, what an idea!

Etienne frowned. He felt sure his mother was holding back the truth. and this lie hurt him. Deep down, he could not stop himself thinking of her as a vulnerable and innocent child, and himself as her only protector. He was afraid she might suffer an irreparable disappointment. This Maxime Joubert, what did they know about him? What did he hope to gain in exchange for his favours? Marriage? A serious matter. Marion should certainly not marry a man because of a kind of weariness. She turned on the hot water tap and the old, black boiler with its discoloured iron top, roared as if it were ready to collapse under the shock. A faint smell of gas filled the cramped bathroom and mingled with the perfume from the open bottles.

'We must get the plumber in, she said, placing her hands under the thin stream of water.

'How many days will you stay in Lyon? he asked

'Forty eight hours at most. Enough time to see these people, to finalise an agreement with them...

She dried her hands, took a narrow belt, shiny, which was hanging on the back of a chair, and buckled it quickly around her waist:

'Does it look better with or without the belt?

Instead of answering her question, he frowned and said with authority:

'Listen...This is serious...I don't want to stop you starting a new life...

She looked at him blankly with her prominent eyes:

'Starting a new life? But I'm not thinking of starting a new life, my darling!

'Let me finish. If you haven't remarried, I'm sure it's because of me.

'No.

'Why, then?

'Let's say that a first experience has been enough to put me off.

Etienne looked down, as if suddenly ill at ease. He was six when his parents had divorced, for reasons which, even today, seemed difficult to understand. Since that time, not once had he been given the opportunity to see his father. Having left Paris, Louis Martin had settled in Cauterets and had remarried a woman who had little money. Not long after the landing of the allied troops in France, he was to die in an accident. According to Marion's story, he was riding a bicycle when an army lorry had shot across the road, struck him and thrown him against a tree.

'You mustn't think that all men are like him, continued Etienne. Marriage isn't necessarily a bad thing.

'Not necessarily.

This M. Joubert, I don't know him, but he's probably a decent sort of bloke...If he loves you and you love him, I shall be the first to tell you to marry him. But if you are simply giving in to weariness, if you are fearful of the future, well, please, trust me. You are not alone. You are *no longer* alone... I've passed my philosophy baccalauréat. In three years I shall have my law degree. I shall be a barrister in Paris I shall be earning. You will be able to take it easy...I shall give you a wonderful life...

As he spoke, the words were catching in his throat. He was feeling stupidly emotional. Embarrassed, he coughed in order to speak more clearly and continued in a conciliatory tone:

'How old is he? Forty-five? Fifty? You need a man at least seven years older than you...

At these words, she slammed the window shut, as if she were afraid the neighbours might hear their conversation. Her whole face was trembling, pink and warm, and there was an aggressive light in her eyes. She was breathing jerkily. She said:

'That's enough, Etienne. I tell you again that M Joubert is less interested in me than in my little dressmaking business. It's a difficult struggle for a woman on her own...the bills, the payment deadlines... Among my contacts are several friends with whom I happen to spend the evening from time to time. Never about any of them have you spoken to me about ...about...feelings...about marriage...And then suddenly...It's ridiculous...

'M Joubert is not like the others, he said.

'Why?

'You need to ask yourself that question. You have only known him for two months and, in two months, you have changed your appearance. With the others, you haven't changed your appearance. Besides, look, you're getting angry. Marion, Marion, why are you getting angry?

From the time he had lived alone with his mother, he had taken to calling her by her first name.

'I am not getting angry, she said. But you irritate me with your questions. You are too inclined to forget that....

'That you are my mother and that I owe you respect? he exclaimed, cheerfully.

He was taller than her by a head. As he looked down at her, she seemed so slight, so pretty, that it worried him.

'Exactly, she said.

And suddenly, and quite unexpectedly, they burst out laughing, standing one in front of the other, united by the knowledge of a happy collusion. He embraced her, showered her with kisses, on her cheeks, on her neck, and she struggled and groaned:

'Etienne! You're spoiling my hair. I shall look like a mad woman.

'You can tell M. Joubert that it's your son's fault.

'He won't believe me.

'He will be jealous?

'Of course not. Why should he be? Oh! You annoy me...

She escaped from his embrace, took a comb and passed it through her hair:

'Now look what you've done!...I'm in a right state!...You're making me late...

'Don't do anything, he said. I shall tidy your mess. Quickly, off you go...

He was putting the tops back on the perfume bottles, re-screwing the top of the toothpaste tube, tidying the pots of face cream on the shelf above the washbasin:

'What a concoction!

'Necessary at my age, she said.

'Do be quiet! You are beautiful and M. Joubert is extremely lucky!

She took a carnation, which was soaking in a tooth glass, and held it to her bodice:

'Here?

'No, he said. A little higher and more to the right. There. Perfect.

He picked up a pin, which was lying on the floor, handed it to Marion and asked:

'What time will you be back this evening?

'Probably about eight. Lay the table before I get back. We shall have a cold meal...

Already she was opening the bathroom door and slipping through to the cool, dark landing. He followed her, breathing in her perfume, listening to the rustling of her dress. Behind the glazed double door of the lounge-dining room, a sewing machine was methodically cutting through the silence. A woman's voice cried out:

'You're going out, Miss Marion?

'Yes, Suzanne. Don't worry about me. We shall make a decision tomorrow about the bolero...

And, turning towards her son, she added quietly:

'I don't want to see her. I would be there for an hour. She's such a talker! What are you going to do while I'm away?

'Read.

'Read? Always reading! Incorrigible philosopher!

She ruffled his hair with a boyish gesture, planted a kiss on his cheek, opened the landing door, and was quickly gone; just the sound of her pointed toes, striking the stairs, as if they were the keys of a piano.

At once he found himself alone, and at a loose end, in the hall, where a mirror shone between the outline of two coats hanging parallel to each other. The noise of the sewing machine was suddenly deafening. Then there was silence: Mme Marthe was cutting the thread, getting the material to pivot. When the machine started up again, Etienne felt as if a needle was rapidly piercing his very being with a thousand holes. "Later, he thought, when I'm a lawyer, I shall throw these dressmakers out and install my office in this room. Our house will become a man's house. That's how it should be." His hand hesitated on the fluted brass door handle. He pushed the door open. Fierce autumn sunlight was setting ablaze the dining room, with its brown wooden furniture. Fourteen cockerels were painted on fourteen plates, fixed to the wall. A huge chandelier, constructed with bowls, little candle holders and artificial foliage, hung from the ceiling like a sea monster floating just below the surface of the water. The stupid chattering of the sewing machine made the floor tremble. Mme Marthe and Mlle Suzanne were working there in a chaotic mess of ragged material, bobbins, scissors and fashion magazines. The ladies had placed their hats on the mantelpiece, on either side of a metal clock with small marble columns. They did not look up as the intruder came in. But Mlle Suzanne, her mouth bristling with pins, said:

'Well. M Etienne, still at home? That's no good for a young man of your age!

Leaning over the table, she was trimming a piece of blue silk with little white flowers. The scissors bit into the material with the noise of snow cracking. The air smelt of female perspiration and fabric glue. It was warm. Mme Marthe was old and round shouldered. You could see the talcum powder on her face. She had dark, Spanish eyes and her hands were deformed by rheumatism. Mlle Suzanne was thin and blond and her nose was glistening. She wore a transparent blouse of a thin mauve material. Contemplating Etienne, who was saying nothing, she murmured again, to encourage him to break his silence:

'Incredibly hot, isn't it. Even for midsummer it's unusual. I'm pouring with sweat. When you think of all those lucky devils on holiday by the sea!...

She hitched up, under her blouse, the strap of her petticoat, which had slipped down. A brief smile crossed her lips. "Against this wall, Etienne thought, I shall place my bookcase. A large table with a telephone. Another table where I can study my clients' files. On the right side a filing cabinet for their addresses."

'I'm finishing this one and I'm off, continued Mlle Suzanne. It's gone six! I would like to have spoken to your mum about Mme Piat's bolero. But she seemed in a hurry.

Etienne looked away and said:

'Yes, she had a meeting. If you want to go...

'We're going, we're going!

He had the impression that the two women were better informed than he was on the relationship of his mother with this unknown man. "I wonder if they have already slept together", he thought. He suddenly blushed. He left the room without turning back. Behind the door, once again closed, he thought he heard whispering and laughter:

"Are they making fun of me or mum? But perhaps they aren't making fun of anyone? They often laugh between themselves. It's normal that mum should think of remarrying. One of these days she will introduce me to this M Joubert. Rather a plump individual, greying a little, rather opinionated. In the textile business, a member of several boards. I can see him now. My father was only the manager of a local cinema, in the twelfth arrondissement. A man should not be judged by his job. If Marion marries Maxime Joubert, we shall become friends. Because of her. Only because of her."

He sighed, not with sadness, and was pleased to return to his room. A narrow crack ran across the chalky material of the ceiling. The wallpaper was patterned with boring vegetation: washed out bindweed and trailing greenery. The carpet was threadbare. There were books everywhere: on the shelves of a bookcase, under the cupboard, on top of the cupboard, on the bed, under the bed. Enthroned on the mantelpiece was a plaster bust, the eyes and hair of which had been painted with Indian ink. On each side of the window two glass fronted display cases served as transparent prisons to huge butterflies with green mottled wings. A pin fixed each one, at its centre, to a rectangle of white cardboard. Etienne picked up from the table a slim pamphlet with a salmon pink cover. It was the order of ceremony for the last Prize Giving. The introductory speech had been given this year by the philosophy teacher, M Thuillier. Etienne opened the booklet at the first page:

> In the disorder of the modern world, in the aftermath of a bloody and confused conflict, with possibly an even more incredible blow to came, it is towards you, young people, that hope turns, the hope of those whose mission it is to preserve, come what may, the fragile values of culture, research and freedom. Every task, however absurd, however condemned to failure, can be undertaken with joy. There is no destiny which cannot be overcome by pride. The man who wants truly to be a man must accept the constraints of his situation, and must accept them as so many advantages characteristic of his human condition.

Etienne turned over a few pages:

> Prize for overall excellence: Martin (Etienne)...First Prize for

Philosophy: Martin (Etienne), Second Prize for Philosophy: Biosque (Clement)...First Prize for Physics and Chemistry: Palaiseau (Bernard)... Second Prize for Physics and Chemistry: Martin (Etienne),...First Prize for History and Geography: Martin (Etienne)...

A smile played on his lips. He felt truly the best. In everything. Nothing could stand in his way when he entered the adult world. He passed his hand over his cheek, where his beard was beginning to grow. For some time he had been shaving every two days in order to encourage the growth of this down like hair. His chest swelled with such strength that he suddenly wished he had before him an opponent to fight, an antagonist to disarm in debate, a woman to seduce. The wardrobe mirror reflected the image of a tall, thin boy, with a bulbous forehead, plenty of blond hair, the wide, supple mouth of an orator. A fluid light moved in his green eyes, centred on their tiny black pupils. He did not look like his mother. Whom, then, did he resemble? Louis Martin? Marion claimed not. But Etienne suspected that she was not telling the truth: "What can it matter to her that I look like my father? Does she hate him that much? She would have every right, after what she has suffered through him. Anyway, I hate him. I hate him and I pity him. Poor stupid fool!" He repeated angrily, under his breath :

'Poor, stupid fool!

Having been, from earliest childhood, estranged from his father, Etienne found it difficult to believe that this person had really existed: receding hair, a short, slender nose, a thin moustache. It was impossible to give life to these features, to imagine a gesture, a voice, from this ghost refusing to co-operate.

Etienne sat down on the bed and a book, dislodged as the bed sank under him, fell onto the carpet. It was *Les Confessions* by Jean-Jacques Rousseau[1]. Its spine was broken and the print very small. He picked the volume up and leafed through it casually:

> I am aware of my soul and I know men. I am not made like any I have seen. I dare to believe that I am not made like any who exist. If I am not more worthy, at least I am different...

Page after page, he allowed the intimate music of this revelation to penetrate him. Immersed in his reading, he was forgetting the passage of time and the changing light. The harmonious unhappiness of Jean-Jacques Rousseau was becoming the very soul of his own being. When his eyes became tired on account of the tightly printed lines he took another book: "The world as willpower and representation", by Schopenhauer[2]. It was as if Rousseau's self pity was prolonged through the writings of the German philosopher: "With its disappointed hopes, and accidents which upset all its plans, life carries the imprint of a nature very likely to inspire disgust". Etienne liked this sentence. He intended to copy it into his notebook. But as he was getting up, the telephone rang. "It's Marion calling. She will not be coming home for dinner." A morbid foreboding was directing his steps towards the hall. He picked up the receiver.

'Hello! Etienne Martin? It's Palaiseau.

Bernard Palaiseau was a classmate, whose company held not the slightest interest for him. Yet, after being alone for a long time, Etienne was happy to hear a friendly voice.

'What are you up to, these days? asked Palaiseau.

'Nothing special, said Etienne. And what about you? I thought you were due to leave Paris for the holidays.

'Change of plan. My father's broke. We are all tightening our belts. We could meet up.

'If you like.

'When?

Etienne worked out that in two days' time, Marion would have left for Lyon. He did not want to commit himself before then.

'Thursday, he replied, I'm free then.

'I'll come round early in the morning. We'll go for a bike ride.

'Fine.

He hung up. The prospect of a bicycle ride with Palaiseau was pleasant enough. "On the one hand Bernard Palaiseau and, on the other, Arthur Schopenhauer. Isn't it odd that I am attracted, in turn, by these two opposed poles of life? Can I truly be myself, whilst accepting that my mind has such a strange divergence of inspiration? If this carries on, I shall have the impression that I am reading Palaiseau and pedalling with Schopenhauer." He smiled at this preposterous idea and promised himself that he would convey it to his friend. In the flat above, a child was pulling a toy cart and colliding with furniture. Mme Marthe and Mlle Suzanne had finished work and left the house. It was time to lay the table. Etienne went into the dining room, which had reverted to its domestic state. A cloth covered the sewing machine. From the avenue de Tourville there arose the noise of a hot city in high summer. Etienne unfolded the table cloth, set out two plates, one opposite the other, and stood still, thinking. One day, would there perhaps be three plates, three places set on this same table? "Certainly not. He's well off. We'll go and live at his house. Scarcely had he conceived this idea, that he vehemently rejected it: She will go, if she wants. Not me. I have my own point of view." He placed the bottle of red wine on a coaster made of cork. The fourteen cockerels kept a mocking eye on him. His hands were working in the present and his mind in the future: "If she gets back before eight o'clock, it means that she will not marry him. If she gets back after eight o'clock...If I can hold these two knife rests balanced on top of each other, it means that I shall get on well with my future step father. If not...If the bus sounds its horn as it passes under the window..."

A barely perceptible smell of coal came into the room. The clock on the mantelpiece struck eight o'clock. Shortly afterwards, a key turned in the lock. Etienne rushed into the hall. She said: 'I haven't kept you waiting too long? He did not reply and concentrated all his attention on this face, which, in the dusk, seemed to re-create the light of the day. Her eyes, her mouth, three points of happiness. It pained him. The red carnation on her bodice was crumpled, faded, and hung its head.

'Well, he said, when are you leaving?

'Tomorrow evening.

'On the train?

'Of course. M Joubert is sure that I shall be successful with these gentlemen. If that is the case, I shall employ a third worker, someone who specialises in looser fitting clothes.

She was speaking and he let her continue, while touching her shoulder, breathing in her perfume, looking at her forehead and her hair.

Chapter Two

Two rings at the bell: it was the post. Etienne opened the door. The caretaker was standing in the doorway, a bundle of envelopes in her hand. She asked:

'Is that one of your friends who came by bike just now?

'Yes.

'You must tell him that it is not permitted to leave bicycles in the entrance hall. It causes an obstruction. There's a special place, at the back of the yard.

'He didn't know, said Etienne. Anyway, we shall be going in a moment

The caretaker, thickset and pale, breathless, looked at him reproachfully:

'You understand, if everybody left their bicycles in the entrance hall...

Etienne took the letters, smiled, closed the door again. Mme Marthe's voice called out:

'What is it?

'The post, said Etienne.

'Oh, I see, said Mme Marthe.

The sewing machine continued its regular humming, behind the glass door. Etienne wanted to read the addresses on the envelopes. But it was too dark in the entrance hall. He went back into his room, where Palaiseau was waiting for him, sitting in an armchair, his head thrown back, his feet spread wide.

'I thought I heard her moaning about my bike, he said. They're all the same. Their dream is to have only impotent old men as tenants....

He yawned vigorously and held out both hands in front of him, his fingers linked together. The sun, shining through the open window, lit up his thick mop of hair, which was the colour of mahogany, and his chubby cheeks, which were covered in freckles. An American style jacket, beige at the back and blue in the front, hung, like a sack, on his shoulders. His yellow leather shoes, with their prominent stitches, shone brightly.

'You've got great shoes. said Etienne.

'I've pinched them from my father. We're the same size. It's very convenient.

'Yes.. of course...

While he was speaking, Etienne slipped the envelopes from one hand to the other to check who had sent them.

'They're for you, all those letters? asked Palaiseau.

'Not at all. For my mother.

Brochures, the telephone bill, a post card with a photograph of the promenade des Anglais, in Nice. On the back, these few words written in spidery handwriting: *Much love and lots of kisses – Daisy*. It was one of Marion's customers. Suddenly, Etienne's eyes alighted on a square envelope with the postmark Agadir-Morocco. The letter was addressed to him.

'Well? muttered Palaiseau. Are we going? It's already ten o'clock. If you want to cycle in the Bois, we're going to have to get a move on.

'Wait a bit, said Etienne.

He opened the envelope and drew out a sheet of paper, with scalloped edges, in the form of parchment. The handwriting was not familiar to him. From one side of the page to the other ran clumsy letters, shaky, leaning over as if struck by a gust of wind:

Sir,
I do not know you but fate has decreed that we have a common grief. I
am your father's second wife. After his death, I made an official request
to the clerk of the court, and, in my capacity as widow, those gentlemen
sent me his personal effects, objects with no monetary value, which
were removed from Louis Martin. Not a great deal, certainly, but better
than nothing. I have religiously treasured these remains of the deceased
until the present day. Now I am ill. The doctors say that I will get better.
However, I do not think so. As I have not got long to live, I want to
put my affairs in order. My late husband often spoke to me about you.
Several times he wanted to see you again, at the time when things were
turning out so badly for him. But you were still only a very young boy
and your mother was against the idea. I do not judge her. She had her
reasons. Nevertheless, I thought it right to send you, through the post,
the few souvenirs of our loved one, which are in my possession. You will

receive the parcel separately. I hope they will bring you pleasure. And it
is with this thought that I sign myself,

Yours sincerely,
Mme Louis Martin, widow

'Nothing serious? asked Palaiseau.

'No, said Etienne, at least I don't think so....family matters....

He re-read the letter carefully. The idea of receiving items which
had belonged to his father gave him only a slight satisfaction; probably
a wallet or a pipe, which the traffic police had found on Louis Martin's
body after the accident. It was of no importance. Etienne picked up the
envelope, looked at the stamp: Agadir...He imagined sand, palm trees,
mosques, white houses, and also a woman alone, common, old before her
time, writing by the light of a lamp, sniffing back her tears. A degree of
pity touched his heart for this correspondent of no importance.

'Come on, look lively, said Palaiseau.

Etienne stuffed the letter into his jacket pocket and pushed his friend
towards the door.

They pedalled for a long time, side by side, in the green lanes which
smelled of dust. Occasionally a car would overtake them, with a roar of
speed, and Bernard Palaiseau would shout: "Bastard!" or "Capitalist!" and
Etienne would laugh gently, purely out of kindness. But, deep down, he
wasn't enjoying it. Leaning over his handlebars, his head thrust down
into his shoulders, he was thinking all the time about Marion, Maxime
Joubert, the letter; and a feeling of bitterness weighed on his heart. As
a reaction against this numbing sadness, he increased his speed and
outstripped his friend. The wind was whistling at his ears, and, like
a flexible rod, whipping the grass. Between his powerful legs the cycle
moved rapidly ahead, vibrating, metallic. Warmth rose from his calves to
his stomach. Behind him he heard Palaiseau yelping:

'Wait for me! You've....you've got stronger muscles than me!...It's not
fair!...

"I've lost him", Etienne said to himself. He felt a justifiable pride and
carried on pedalling at top speed, along the road which ran beside the
edge of the Auteuil race course.

When he stopped at last, out of breath, in a lane off the main road,
Bernard Palaiseau had disappeared. Etienne spotted a lawn with a quiet,

shady corner, leaned his bike against a tree trunk and lay out on the grass to get his breath back. He was lying on his back, his hands crossed under his neck. Beneath his shirt, which was soaked in sweat, he felt the coldness of the earth. Above him, filtered by the leaves, the sunlight was constantly moving. "It's funny, thought Etienne, that this woman should write to me in this way, not knowing me, and should send me items I haven't asked for. Marion is wrong never to speak to me about my father. Whatever grudge she might bear towards Louis Martin, she ought to remember that I am his son and, as such, I have a right to information. I don't even have a photograph at home, not even a letter. She burned everything. And it has to be a stranger who takes it upon herself to bring to life for me the memory of a man whose name I bear."

Half closing his eyes, he brought to mind the smell of tobacco, a manly smile, the caress of a heavy hand in his hair. What else? This far off time had left him only the odd, colourless trace. A few paltry images, always the same, responded to his attempts to remember. It was Christmas Eve or the New Year. His father was lifting him up in his arms, to show him the window of a department store, full of dolls, trains, boats. Around them, kids shouted out in the darkness, which smelled of frost and burnt sugar. Above the crowd, Etienne did not want to come back down. His mother was getting angry. His father was saying: "It's alright, Marion, I am not tired." One evening he had taught Etienne how to fill a pipe. At table, it was not unusual for him to make jokes or to pretend, in order to amuse the child, to eat his soup with a fork. There was nothing, it seemed, that would lead one to think he was a nasty man.

What had gone on between him and Marion? Every time that Etienne had attempted to question his mother about the early years of her marriage, about the divorce, the departure and death of Louis Martin, she had avoided his questions with a sad expression. Obviously she wanted to forget this disappointing experience. Etienne vaguely remembered Marion's face, drawn and glistening with tears. Doors slammed. A fist banged on the table. A woman's voice shouted: "You've got no right, Louis..." Then silence, emptiness. They moved to another flat, another district. A sewing machine appeared in the house. There were no longer any men's clothes in the cupboards. The smell of tobacco had vanished. Mme Marthe and Mlle Suzanne were bringing into the dining room their paraphernalia of scissors and cut material, their distinctive perfume and their chatter. Marion was reverting to her maiden name and becoming Mme Loiselet. It was the end of an era, of a reign. It still surprised Etienne that this family upheaval had caused him so little suffering. If he was thinking about it today, it was because of the letter he had received. And also, of course, because Marion was thinking of remarrying. Why not Maxime Joubert? "If I had loved my father, if I had respected his memory, such an idea would have seemed sacrilegious. But he walked out on us, he caused Marion unhappiness. The fact that he is dead does not change anything...." He imagined a bicycle crushed against a tree, wrecked, shattered, with useless wheels and twisted handlebars. A human body, bloodstained, lying on the road. This vision only brought about within him a moderate curiosity. "He did not deserve a different death. If he had lived, I would have sought him out to express my disdain, my anger." The tinkling of a bicycle bell broke into his thoughts.

'Hey, I am over here, shouted Etienne.

Bernard Palaiseau climbed over the wire which surrounded the lawn and threw his bike on the grass:

'You!... I'll get you for this!..

He was finding it difficult to speak, his voice was lifeless, his face puffy with exhaustion. He dropped down heavily next to Etienne and closed his eyes, as if he was about to go to sleep. Not far away, to the left, some kids were playing football. A young woman, wearing a white dress, walked along the lane. She was pushing a pram which squeaked with every turn of its wheels. Bernard Palaiseau took a handkerchief from his pocket and placed it over his burning face. Only his red hair was visible. Where his nose was, the handkerchief rose to a point. Where his mouth was, there was a hollow, where the material, slightly damp, was quivering like a membrane.

'You are going to be even hotter like that, said Etienne.

'Not at all, said Palaiseau. It helps me rest. I need time to recover.

'If you had a decent bike, you would have kept up with me.

'No. I haven't got your lungs. I am sure you would beat Maroussel in a sprint.

'You're joking!

They discussed, somewhat harshly, the sporting qualities of Maroussel, who, three times, had come top in Gymnastics.

'Maroussel is not particularly talented, said Palaiseau, He's just good at using his muscles. But you are good both physically and mentally. And, believe me, Martin, my dear old mate, that is very rare.

Etienne blushed with pleasure and murmured, without giving it any thought:

'Oh, I don't know. We are what we are...

Then they referred to other friends, listing the virtues and defects of each. Few of the boys were spared Palaiseau's acerbic criticism. To hear him talk, of all the class, only Etienne Martin was worthy of any consideration.

'I've spoken a lot about you to my parents, he said. One day you must come home with me, I'll introduce you...

'What do your parents do? asked Etienne.

'My father is a chemical engineer. He's a great bloke. We get on very well. On Sunday mornings we play billiards together.

When his friends spoke to him about their fathers, Etienne felt a sense of inferiority. It seemed to him that, in the structure of his personal universe, something was missing, a strong voice, a vigilant eye, a presence, the authority of a mature man. His own milieu was strictly feminine and cosy. Everything was roundness, perfume, comfortable warmth. He had lived within it for years, with an unconscious regret for manliness. Once again, he regretted his parents' divorce, the meaningless death of this father he had barely known.

'My father is dead, he said.

'I know, said Palaiseau.

Etienne imagined M. Palaiseau playing billiards with his son.

'And your mother is in dressmaking? Palaiseau continued. She must make a lot of money.

'Bad mistake, said Etienne in a serious tone. The competition is fierce. Some customers don't pay. If you knew how keen I am to get away from it, to earn my own living!

'You still want to be a lawyer?

'Yes.

'I'm told it takes many years of training. Still, you have all the qualities you need to make a name for yourself. You have presence, you are eloquent. In future years, if I have to go to court, it's you I will choose to defend me.

'Why?

'Because I have confidence in you, said Palaiseau.

Etienne started laughing, flattered, embarrassed. His hands went weak.

'You have confidence in me?

'Certainly. said Palaiseau. In everything you do, you are successful. Your philosophy homework, I would like to copy it, to keep a record of it. And then, you're a good looking bloke!

'You exaggerate!

'No, I don't. I assure you, you're very handsome. You will have all the girls you want. That's important in a career. You get on through women. Who do you look like, your father or your mother?

'I don't know, said Etienne.

'He hesitated a while, then added:

'My father...

'Me too, said Palaiseau. Only I'm not good looking. I know and I don't care. Later on I shall go into business. I shall be a businessman and you will be my legal advisor. Between the two of us, we'll make a vast fortune!

There was then a silence between them, which was heightened by the rustling of leaves above them and the shouts of children quarrelling. Etienne thought that he found Palaiseau, by turns, unpleasant and likeable. "He likes me more than I like him. He admires me. Yet, I cannot admire him. Am I really a superior being? Yes, indeed! I shall surprise them all. I will control my destiny. People will talk about me..." He reached out with his hand and touched the pedal of his bike, which was resting against a tree. The pedal turned on its axle. Palaiseau removed the handkerchief which was covering his face and said:

'So, your mother receives customers who come to the house to try on dresses, in the living room?

'Yes, said Etienne.

'And where are you during this time?

'Where do you think I am? In my bedroom, of course!

'You've never seen anything?

'What?

Palaiseau's face creased in a mocking grimace, his eyes no longer visible. He whispered:

'I was thinking that you would perhaps have seen women...women in their underwear or completely naked...

'No, said Etienne.

'Yet, you're well placed...As for me, in the house opposite, the part where the maids live...He sniggered into his fist. Etienne glanced at him in surprise.

'She's a redhead like me. We wave at each other.

'Have you already tried...?

'No, replied Palaiseau, I'm waiting to find something better. My father says that one of these days he will introduce me to a lovely little girl friend. My father is very modern. He believes that the first time is important...

Etienne began to turn the pedal of his bike again. Now he was also thinking of this "first time" and tried to imagine the face of the one who would come out of the crowd for him. The thought of this physical union with a being so different from him, in body and soul, in her dress and movements, filled him with an astonishment, which was pleasant.

'Sometimes. at night, I can't sleep, said Palaiseau. I imagine that a woman is sitting astride my chest. Her skirt is covering my face.

He picked up his handkerchief again and threw it onto his face:

'Like this...Exactly like this. And underneath it I breathe in. That arouses me...

Etienne's buttocks, painful from the saddle. were becoming hard, uncomfortable. He changed position and lay on his side.

'You're the first person I've told that to, admitted Palaiseau.

His breath was making the handkerchief quiver. It was like the heart of a chicken beating beneath this thin and dirty screen. A feeling of disgust suffused Etienne's whole being. He did not like the vulgar way in which his friend spoke of sex. Having always lived in close proximity to Marion, he could not prevent himself from thinking that every smutty joke, directed against women in general, was an insult to his mother in particular. He had gone with her, the day before, to the station. She had gone off alone. But perhaps Maxime Joubert was waiting for her in Lyon? Suddenly he imagined Marion in a man's arms, and he felt a void filling his chest.

'Do you want us to be close friends? asked Palaiseau.

'Yes, whispered Etienne.

He was not thinking about what he was saying. A football rolled right up to him and he pushed it away moodily with his foot.

'Thank you, monsieur, cried a child's voice.

Etienne found no happiness even in being called "monsieur". For a few seconds it even seemed that a sudden disconnect had occurred in his consciousness. By turns he experienced the sensation that he did not exist and another sensation, no less strange, of being the only living creature on earth. M. Thuillier's teaching had made the whole class familiar with this state of meditation, which the teacher called "creative confusion". You half closed your eyes, you held your breath, you imagined climbing from one cloud to another: "Who am I? What is the meaning of life? How must I conduct myself in order to exploit to the full this promise, which is inherently within me?" Having reached this point of dizziness, in your imagination, you tumbled down the steps, four by four, and clung onto your seat, saying "There will be chips for lunch!" or else "Etienne Martin speaking". And a trembling happiness would fill your body, as if you had just avoided an accident.

'You're miles away, said Palaiseau.

'I was thinking, said Etienne.

'About what?

'Nothing...everything...life...

'You mustn't think about life, you must live it, said Palaiseau. Life is for living.

Etienne raised himself on his elbows and whispered:

'Do you really have the feeling of being alive at this moment? Are you exactly what you feel yourself to be? Do you not have the impression that, by pure force of will, you could think yourself into being a bird or a fish? I sometimes wonder what Thuillier thinks about when he is alone with himself. You know that he is writing a philosophical treatise which will cause a sensation? He told me that after the Prize Giving, when we all went for a drink together. It will be entitled: *Measuring nothingness*. We ought to pay him a visit when we're back at school...

'To do what?

'To have a chat with him. He's a nice bloke. He would be delighted.

'Do you have his address?

'Yes: 13, rue de l'Eperon.

'You will have to go on your own, said Palaiseau. Philosophy bores me stiff.

'I thought like you at the beginning of the year. Later on I got hooked on it. Thullier is a trend setter. You can't resist him. What energy! What intelligence! And then, what's great about the bloke is that he treats his pupil like friends. Can you imagine old Ponchon taking us into the Bois de Boulogne to have philosophy lessons in the open air like the ancient Greeks?

Suddenly Etienne wondered, completely objectively, if he would like Marion to have married M. Thuillier. Certainly, M. Thuillier was nothing to look at: big and fat, with a substantial paunch, a puffy face, his eyes covered with thick lenses. But, as soon as he started speaking, you forgot his physical ugliness and his ill-fitting clothes. Almost as a joke, Etienne imagined his mother meeting the philosophy teacher, being charmed by him and rejecting the second rate Maxime Joubert in favour of him. He imagined M. Thuillier moving into the house, sharing Marion's bed, having his meals at the family table. Swelling with importance, round eyed, pink lipped, he would talk philosophy whilst eating his soup. Etienne quivered, as if he had struck his elbow against the furniture. Stars danced in front of his eyes. Palaiseau asked:

'What are you doing this afternoon?

'I don't know, said Etienne. How about you?

'I'm going shopping, with my father.

A mass of leaves and branches bent in the wind above their heads. One by one, Etienne married his mother off to all the men he knew: the headmaster, the deputy head, friends, Victor Hugo[1], Stendhal[2], Jean-Jacques Rousseau, Lamartine[3]. Palaiseau looked at his watch:

'Shall we go back?

'If you want.

'I'm pleased that we've become close friends, said Palaiseau.

They got on their bikes. Palaiseau placed a hand on Etienne's shoulder. They rode for a long time like that, close to each other, together yet apart, without exchanging a word.

On his return home, Etienne had lunch with Mlle Suzanne, who, in Marion's absence, had agreed to do the cooking and have her meals in the house: chicken vol-au-vents and steak in red wine; the dressmaker had excelled herself. In an attempt to please her, Etienne had to eat more than normal. He was swallowing large mouthfuls and Mlle Suzanne was looking at him with sympathy. She said 'If the oven hadn't been broken, I would have made you my own special dessert. You take a quarter litre of milk, a little flour...' Under her transparent mauve blouse, Etienne could see the shape of two ample breasts, held in check by her bra straps. When he got up from the table, his stomach was heavy and his eyelids were closing with tiredness. He took refuge in his bedroom, stretched out on his bed and took from his pocket the letter from Agadir. The words, poorly written, danced about before his eyes. The yellowish paper gave off a perfume of soap.

The parcel arrived by the evening post. It contained an old watch, a wallet and some cuff links.

Chapter Three

Etienne put the case down in the hall, opened the dining room door and said:

'I've prepared a small, cold supper, just in case.

'Thank you, darling, said Marion. But I'm not hungry. I've already eaten in the restaurant car.

Standing in front of the mirror by the front door, she was taking off her hat, her gloves, ruffling the hair on her temples. A gentle weariness was evident in her face. She seemed happy and exhausted.

'How nice to be back home! she went on, stretching her arms in front of her.

During the journey, from the station to home, in the taxi, she had explained to Etienne the results of her trip, as they related to her work. Thanks to M. Joubert's recommendations, the manager of the Alfar Company, had turned out to be especially understanding. From the month of October, this major firm would send to Marion the fabric for manufacture in bulk....

'I've brought you some samples, she said. They are all stunning. You'll see. Open my case..

He started laughing:

'Later, Marion. We've got plenty of time.

And, without listening to her protests, he pushed her into the brightly lit dining room. Two places laid. Cold meat. Some fruit. In the middle of the table, Etienne had placed six pink carnations in a stoneware vase. Marion saw the flowers and, clearly moved, looked at her son:

'Did you do that?

'Yes

'Oh! Etienne, you shouldn't have!

'Be quiet and eat.

'I can no longer refuse, she said, with the pretty smile of a pampered woman.

She sat on a chair, picked a few grapes from the fruit bowl and chewed them in a preoccupied manner. There was a mauve line around her eyes; her lips, without lipstick, were pale. She asked:

'No post?

'Yes, he said, I put it in my bedroom.

'Mme Piat's bolero?

'It was delivered yesterday morning.

'Excellent. And so what have you been doing for the last two days?

'Nothing interesting. I've done some reading. I saw a friend...

He hesitated for a moment and drew from his pocket the letter he had received while Marion had been away.

'Look, he said. Read that. It's a funny business!

She took the piece of paper he was holding out to her, unfolded it and glanced over it. From the very beginning, a small, vertical line appeared between her eyebrows. Pushing her chin forward she muttered:

'This woman is mad!

'She believed she was doing the right thing. Her letter is not, perhaps, very well written, but she's acting in the right spirit.

Marion was not listening to him; she was pursuing her own thoughts:

'Mad! Mad! What right has she got to pester you like this? How dare she write to you, upset you?

'She hasn't upset me...

'Yes, she has, Etienne. She's upsetting you, she's upsetting us. And she knows it. This parcel...this parcel she's talking about, have you received it?

'Yes, he said. Cuff links, a wallet, a watch. Do you want to see them?...

She jumped to her feet. The paper began to tremble between her hands. Her face stiffened with anger, with disgust. Etienne was frightened by the effect that these few words had produced on Marion's features. Probably it would have been better to wait for the next day before speaking to her about the letter. But could he have foreseen that his mother's reaction would be so violent? After a long silence, she said in a muffled tone:

'What have you done with those things?

'I've put them in my table drawer.

'You should not have accepted this parcel, she whispered, throwing the letter onto her plate. You should not..

He did not follow her reasoning, he considered that she was at the mercy of hatred, of absurd fears.

'Look, Marion, don't over dramatise the situation. I could very well have done without these souvenirs, but now that they are here...

'You should throw them away, Etienne.

'Why? Because they belonged to my father?

'Yes.

'It makes no sense! he said, folding his arms. Really, mum, you are not being rational. If divorce proceedings mean that you are no longer Louis Martin's wife, that doesn't stop me from being his son. Whether I like it or not, that is my status, I carry his name. In these circumstances, how could I have completely no interest in him? I am not saying that I love him, that I respect him. But he intrigues me. Look, I hardly know anything about his life. The letter speaks of measures taken with the courts, of a difficult time. What does that mean?

Marion had got up and was walking around the room, her hands held tightly together on her stomach.

'You see, he continued, in a victorious tone, you don't know yourself, or you pretend not to know. Besides, it's obvious enough, every time I refer to my father, you clam up, you shy away...

She stopped, her head erect. The line across her forehead had deepened further. Fine crusts of face powder marked the corners of her lips. Behind her, on the wall, the white centre of a plate shone brightly.

'Your father walked out of our life, your life. You must dismiss him from your memory. I have deliberately destroyed everything which could remind you of him: photographs, letters...

Etienne was dumbfounded by his mother's abnormal behaviour. So much injustice suddenly made him want to take the dead man's side. He shouted:

'You were considerate even to the point of preventing me from seeing him! He was about to die, he wanted to meet me. This woman said so in her latter.

'I can't deny it.

'Why did you do that?

'For your own good.

'That's a poor excuse, Marion. You didn't have the right! You who are so understanding, so fair minded, so gentle! You frighten me...

She took one step towards him, and he was surprised to see her turn pale before his eyes. Her face resembled a plaster bust, with the hair and eyes painted black.

'Marion! Marion! he said, gripped by fear. What's the matter with you? You are hiding something from me. Explain yourself. I need to know.

'What? What do you want to know? she asked. Who he was? How he led his life? Why I was opposed to your meeting him?

Her extreme nervous state agitated her lips, her eyebrows, made the skin of her cheeks tremble.

'A foul individual, she went on, almost screeching. And you, poor Etienne, you are interested in him. You reproach me because I do not speak enough about him. You overflow with gratitude towards this creature who condescends to send you a few souvenirs of Louis Martin!

He stammered:

'It's wrong of you to talk like that, mum. He is dead...

She pushed her head back, and a white semi-circle appeared beneath her large, staring pupils:

'Yes, dead, but not in an accident, Etienne. Your father...your father was executed....

She said no more, as if terrified by her own words. He looked at her, without taking it in, and yet, already slipping into his mind was the consciousness of a disconnect between the life he had lived and the life he was going to live, between the person he thought he was and the person he really was. He repeated:

'Executed?

Marion lowered her eyes:

'Condemned and executed.

'When?

'13th June 1945.

Etienne's body was, by stages, becoming numb. Only in his brain was there now any life. There was a long silence. Marion raised a hand to her forehead and murmured in a deadened voice:

'Darling, I could have hidden the truth from you, for a long time, a very long time. But one of these days you would have learned everything from a stranger. The shock would have been even more painful for you. This stupid letter, this parcel...your stubbornness...it worried me...Tell me that I wasn't wrong to speak to you as I have just done?

'Why did they condemn him?

She shook her head, pitifully.

'What's the point of stirring up this filth?

'You must. You cannot keep silent any longer.

She looked at him now with fear: this tense forehead, these jaws gripped tight under the delicate flesh of her cheeks, these eyes, green, shining, bulging.

'What shall I tell you, my darling? she whispered. The man the judges condemned had nothing in common with the one we knew. As long as he was living with us, I had nothing to reproach him about other than his violence, his laziness, his infidelities. But, after leaving us, he became a...

She regained her breath, closed her eyes and added in a faint voice:

'An appalling person.

There was another long silence. And, suddenly, Etienne let out a cry:

'What? What did he do?

'He committed murder, she said.

He felt that his heart was weakening, was stopping beating, then was starting again wildly, so that blood was coursing everywhere, into his head, into his neck, into his ears. A feeling of stifling heat overtook him. A moment later, he heard a voice – was it his? – which was saying very distinctly:

'Who did he kill?

For a moment she did not reply. Etienne kept his eyes fixed on her, as if he were afraid that she would disappear through a trap door, before revealing her secret.

'Well, speak, mum, he said again.

Her arms fell beside her body. Her shoulders dropped:

'It's difficult...It's painful...You know that, after our divorce, your father had settled in Cauterets...He knew the area well, because he had lived there in his youth...he had opened a cinema, a café...It was during the occupation...People would seek him out to ask him to help them cross over into Spain: members of the Resistance, Jews...He would take them at night, as far as the border.. He killed several of them like that...

'But why? he groaned. Was he on the side of the Germans? Was he working for the Gestapo?

'He was working only for himself, Etienne. What he was interested in was the money that these poor people were taking with them as they fled. He told his neighbours that he had to be away a lot on business. Everybody liked him. They said that he was in the Resistance.

'How did they find out?...

'After the Liberation, the victims' families did some research. Lots of witnesses came forward. Tongues wagged. Your father was arrested, tried...

'And he admitted it?

'Yes.

Etienne sat down on a chair. A great emptiness suddenly surrounded him. He was losing touch with reality. He was falling, flying, he was changing his appearance, his name, his hair, his destiny. With a great effort, he muttered:

'How you must have suffered, mum!

'Forget it, she said, it's nothing, it's in the past...

He looked up:

'It was in the papers, of course

'Yes, Etienne.

'So everybody knows that I am the son of this man?

She smiled:

'Don't worry, darling. Martin is such a common name that no-one has made the connection. We had moved. I had been living alone with you for nearly six years. The trial took place in Tarbes. The provinces are a long way off! Parisians took no interest in the matter. There were a few headlines in the daily newspapers. But the tide of political news washed it all away in two weeks.

'Yet you and my father had many friends in common?

'I drifted away from them.

'They didn't try to see you again at that time?

'No.

He wasn't ready to be convinced:

'So, according to you, nobody knows?

'Nobody.

'The caretaker?'...Mme Marthe?...My teachers?

'Of course not, Etienne...How could they know?

He ran his fingers, splayed and trembling, through his tousled hair:

'You should have warned me before. I am the person most affected. And I knew nothing, nothing...I was taking life as it comes...

She approached him, stood behind his chair and placed her hand on the nape of his neck:

'You were a child, just a young child...

'I was twelve...thirteen...

'Exactly...I still could not confide in you, burden you with such a heavy sorrow... Remember: at that time, I changed your school, to be on the safe side...I made it a point of honour that you should see nothing of my anxiety...And it was like that for years, years...

'So, if I hadn't received this letter, you wouldn't have told me anything?

'Of course I would!...

'When?

She became flustered.

'I don't know...A bit later...At the first opportunity...Some time ago I had already made up my mind to put you in the picture..But, every time I was on the point of speaking, my courage deserted me...

Her voice fell away at the end of the sentence. She placed a hand on her chest. He asked:

'So, these objects that were sent to me are the ones which were kept in the prison office?

'No doubt.

'Yes, that's it, he murmured. A wallet, cuff links, a watch...

He stared fixedly at the bouquet of pink carnations in its stoneware vase. These flowers belonged to a delightful time which had now passed. They had been given to a woman other than Marion by a man other than Etienne. Standing as if on guard between the past and the present, their colour was striking.

'Etienne, she cried, I cannot bear to see you like this, downcast, unhappy! I've hurt you, darling. But it had to be done. Forgive me for being frank, for being brutal. Please promise me not to give any more thought to these horrors.

She leaned towards him, her face distraught, beseeching.

'Of course, mum, he said. Don't worry about me. After all, I barely knew him...

'That's right, she said, in a surge of hope. Let's forget everything, blot everything out. Just the two of us....

She was pressing her son's head against her stomach, cradling him as if lulling him to sleep, covering him with warmth, with tears, with kisses, with hope.

Chapter Four

Etienne was still in bed when the telephone rang. Throwing off the blankets he jumped to his feet, tied the cord of his pyjama trousers and reached the hall just in time to see his mother lift the receiver.

'It's alright, she said, it will be for me.

She was wearing a dressing gown of a pink material with grey stripes. Her face, showing lack of sleep, looked as if it were covered with silk paper. She pressed the receiver close to her cheek:

'Of course it's me. Don't you recognise my voice, Maxime? An excellent trip, and very useful, thanks to you!...

Whilst speaking she was adjusting the edges of her dressing gown on her chest, as if Maxime Joubert's eyes would have reached into the room as surely as his voice.

'A little tired, perhaps...This afternoon?...Of course...

Etienne felt as if he were encroaching and went back into his bedroom. But he was not sleepy. He pushed at the iron shutters, which were stiff and dusty and which creaked open to let in the daylight. The decor had changed its significance during the night. It was as if well tamed furniture had reverted to its wild state. Etienne noticed the Prize Giving list, lying as evidence on the table: *Prize for Overall Excellence: Martin (Etienne), First Prize for Philosophy: Martin (Etienne)*...This first name in brackets. A hard lump formed in his chest, rose into his throat. Marion's voice was silent at the far end of the flat. It was finished. Maxime Joubert was returning, backwards, into the wings. Relieved, Etienne shut himself in the bathroom to wash.

When he went into the kitchen his mother was setting out the breakfast cups on the table, which was covered with a wax cloth decorated with red and white squares. They drank their coffee, ate their bread and butter, sitting opposite each other. Marion was secretly watching her son, as if trying to read, on his features, the consequences of what she had revealed. He felt those maternal eyes scanning his skin, enquiring, anxious.

'Did you sleep well? she asked.

'Certainly. And yourself?

He was forcing himself to be natural in order to calm Marion's fears.

'Me too…I think it will be very warm today…You don't think that the butter is just going off?

He already understood that she would never dare return to their conversation of the day before. Having said what she had to say, her only concern from now on would be to limit the damage. To this son, whom she had both enlightened and wounded, she was desperately pouring out the proven remedies of tenderness and of life carrying on as normal. She was repairing the broken ties, masking the holes, chasing the shadows away. She was doing the housework after the tornado had passed. Etienne was grateful for her diligence. He would not have tolerated her recalling for a second time the appalling memory of his father. To show her that he accepted this convention of silence, he asked for more coffee. An unexpected smile rejuvenated Marion's face:

'Are you still hungry, darling? Oh! how pleased I am to see that!…

She picked up the old white enamel coffee pot, cracked, blackened, with its twisted spout…Her hand was trembling. A small amount of coffee spilled from the cup. Etienne was aware of tears moistening her eyes.

'There you are, my dear, drink your coffee. I'm going to have some more as well.

The sunlight was flooding in through the open window. The set of saucepans, hanging on the wall, was gleaming brightly. Suddenly, Marion placed her hand on Etienne's wrist. A gentle excitement coloured her cheeks. She was breathing quickly. She murmured:

'Etienne…You are not going to believe me…This morning I feel happy…

'Happy?

'Yes. I don't know how to explain it…You are there…Close to me…We are speaking…

She closed her eyes, as if to control her emotion, shook her head, opened her eyes again and said, with a smile:

'It's silly…Pay no attention…Do you have any plans for this afternoon?

He replied without thinking:

'I'm going to see Palaiseau.

'He's a school friend?

'Yes.

'A nice lad?

'Very nice. His father is a chemical engineer...

A sharp point pricked his heart. He could not breathe. "What's happening to me?"

'You've never told me about him, said Marion.

'Maybe not. I'm going to call on him after lunch. He is always at home then. How about you? Are you meeting M Joubert?

She blushed:

'At six o'clock, yes.

He wanted to reply with a joke, but held back. There was a ring at the front door: Mme Marthe and Mlle Suzanne arrived together. They had met in front of the house and were laughing loudly at this coincidence. Marion went with them into the dining room and the three female voices enlivened the emptiness. Etienne got up, went over to the window. An old yellowing newspaper was lying on the tiles in front of the stove. He read a title by chance: *In the USA the atomic bomb is already considered an outdated weapon*...Etienne pushed the newspaper away with his foot. Something cold and heavy formed a blockage in his chest. He felt in a hurry to return to his bedroom. But, when he was in front of his study table, the fact that he had nothing to do frightened him. The sewing machine was humming, then flying away and stopping to get its breath back. Marion was saying:

'No, Suzanne, you must definitely drop this waist. A plunging effect, you understand? As we did for Mme Piat.

Two rings of the bell: it was the caretaker. Three rings of the bell: the housekeeper. Then a customer came, whose piercing voice dominated all the others. Etienne picked up again *Les Confessions* of Jean-Jacques Rousseau.

> Passions were followed by depression; my boredom turned into sadness; I would cry and sigh for no reason; I would feel my life escaping from me without having experienced it...

The book slipped from his hands onto the floor.

There, in the dining room, the customer was saying:

'No, Madame Loiselet, you must change these buttons. I want them in the same material as the dress. And this box pleat, I assure you that it will not hang straight!

Once again, the telephone:

'Hello? Daisy? How nice of you to send me a card! Yes certainly, your suit is ready. Come and try it on at three o'clock!

Etienne threw himself on the bed and blocked his ears with his fingers. The house had become a shop, a hive, a henhouse, a theatre. Several times Marion came into the room, in a flash, to see what her son was doing. As soon as he heard his mother's footstep in the hall, he would change his position, pick up a book, pretend to read. Each time she left, he would lie down again and close his eyes.

*

The periodicals room in the National Library was bathed in a milky light, which flowed down from the ceiling onto the walls, which were covered with dark bindings which resembled armour plating. Around the study tables, the readers, seated at regular intervals, as in a refectory, bent their heads over their portion of text. In front of each one, a journal rested, wide open, on a sloping support. The silence was broken, from time to time, only by the rustling of a page being turned, the sound of someone coughing briefly, a door opening or closing, or the heavy footstep of the library attendant. Etienne had taken his place between a girl who was concentrating fiercely on the *Report of the French Astronomical Society,* and an elderly, moustachioed gentleman, bent and kindly, who was consulting the complete collection of *Assorted Butters.*

'Are you still waiting? said the elderly gentleman. It takes a long time to get served. Especially during the holiday period...

'Yes, said Etienne.

And he looked away, for he was not at all keen to get into conversation with his neighbour. Briefly, he regretted giving up his cycle ride with Palaiseau. Perhaps the librarian could not find the newspapers which Etienne had asked for? Perhaps the year 1945 had been sent for rebinding? In order to calm his anxiety, he forced himself to look at the small ink stains which marked the wood of the table. There were seven, set out more or less like the stars of the Great Bear. The girl snapped shut her handbag. The old gentleman blew his nose.

'And there you are, said the library attendant, *France Soir,* 1945.

Etienne gave a start. The library attendant laid on the table a heavy book bound in cloth.

'Thank you, Etienne murmured.

The attendant walked away.

'At last, said the old gentleman. About time too!

Etienne forced a smile and placed both hands on the book. He hesitated to open it, as if, by this very gesture, he would risk liberating some dark power, which had been held in check. Around him the silence was growing more intense, more solemn, more terrible. Finally, with a brisk movement, he opened the cover of the volume. Thick letters, pictures as black as soot, a flood, an avalanche, a swarm of words. He was turning the pages in feverish haste: 15th April, 17th April, 20th April.. Suddenly, it was as if a whip struck his eyes. His own name jumped out at his face: *Martin!* He looked at his neighbours to the left and to the right. The old gentleman had begun reading again. The girl also. Everything was calm. Etienne bent over the printed page, the lines of which were quivering like a procession of ants.

"From our special correspondent in Tarbes. Today Louis Martin answers for his crimes before the Assize Court...

Beneath this headline, black with funereal ink, was spread out the photograph of a slim man, nervous, hunted. Etienne recognised his father, and a wave of heat rose to his cheeks. There he was, feature by feature, the person whom he still remembered. The one who, in former times, would play with his son, embrace him, kiss him, speak to him in a friendly, lively voice. His everyday companion. Yet, something demonic had hollowed out the flesh of his face. His eyes, wide open, expressed hatred, powerlessness. He had not shaved. His collar lay open at his scrawny neck. Both hands were leaning on the back of a chair. And you could see his handcuffs. It seemed to Etienne that his father was looking at him personally through a moving mist. The world crumbled, with its books, its windows, its bald heads, its tables and its circular clock. Time was running backwards. Nothing had been decided, concluded, executed...

'A hostile murmur greets the entrance of the murderer into the dock. Tall and thin, arrogant, distinguished, the accused looks at the people in the court with a calm disdain. I watch him. I wonder what can be going through his mind. Around me people shuffle, fan themselves with folded newspapers. It is in a tense, anguished atmosphere that the very eminent presiding judge of Saulieu proceeds to the business of establishing his identity. The clerk of the court reads out the accusation. We recall the details of this matter that have been recounted in this very court...

Etienne leaned back against his chair. Large drops of sweat were running down his forehead. He drew his handkerchief from his pocket and vigorously wiped his face.

'It's hot, sighed the old gentleman.

'M Martin, says the presiding judge of Saulieu, you have heard the charges which have been levelled against you. You are now going to be particularly attentive in following the proceedings. Clerk, will you call the witnesses...

The bottom of the page was torn. The article continued on the last page:

When they announce, in front of him, the name Gerard Metivier, Louis Martin starts, the muscles of his face contract. A reaction readily understandable, seeing that Gerard Metivier is the only one who escaped the killing. Left for dead, he was able to get away and he will testify against the murderer.

'In front of the presiding magistrate, continues the presiding judge of Saulieu, you have admitted murdering two people, M and Mme Leon Wolff, grocers, residents of Cauterets, but you have denied involvement in the murder of Edouard Fleck, of 17 rue Caulaincourt, Paris. Do you adhere to your pleas?

You could hear a pin drop. Finally Louis Martin says in a barely audible voice:

'Yes, sir.

Something became detached, fell inside Etienne's chest. His vision became blurred.

The presiding judge of Saulieu leafs through his dossier.

'Following the detailed examination which has been undertaken, it transpires that the murders of which you stand accused before the Court were committed under the following circumstances: after discussing the cost of the journey with your future victims, you would arrange to meet them late at night on the Cambasque plateau. From there you would guide them, via steep paths, towards an isolated and wild looking spot, where you could act without fear of being seen. But, according to your submission, you had carried out thirteen trips to the border without the slightest incident. You were helping some of them escape from France and killing others. Why?

Louis Martin shudders as if emerging from long drowsiness and murmurs:

'I had my reasons.

'I shall tell you why he acted like that! cried the counsel for the prosecution. Those he had guided safely, from them he secretly had good references sent back, which he used to recruit new victims. Far from exonerating the accused, this manner of going about his business bears witness to the Machiavellian nature of a deeply perverted soul.

M Alexis Houssepard, Louis Martin's defending counsel, leaps up in a flurry of black sleeves and frilly white shirt:

'Your Honour, I protest in the most formal manner against an interpretation of the facts which is biased against my client...

Groans of protest rise from the public gallery. The presiding judge threatens to have the court evacuated. Then, with calm at last restored, he turns to Louis Martin:

'M Martin, will you tell us what the motives of your crimes were? You have admitted to the examining judge that, for you, it was not a question of political revenge. From what you say, you were neither a supporter of collaboration nor of the Resistance. Is that correct?

'That is correct, your honour, says Louis Martin.

'There remains, therefore, only one possible motive, and that is the one held by the prosecution: theft. You killed in order to steal...

Louis Martin looks up. His eyes are gleaming like splinters of glass. He says in a hoarse voice:

'No.

'Yet, continues the presiding judge, when the bodies of M and Mme Wolff were exhumed, buried by you in the very spot where you had struck them down, neither money nor jewels were found on them.

Shrugging his shoulders, Louis Martin dismisses this assertion:

'What does that prove? Someone else could have robbed them afterwards...

'So why would you have killed them?

'I have already told the examining judge, Louis Martin replies in an insolent tone. In 1941, Leon Wolff had reported me to the police for dealing on the black market. Because of him, I almost went to prison. Besides, he was hanging round my wife. I didn't like that. From that time I had resolved to take my revenge. When the Germans crossed the demarcation line, he came to ask me, all sheepish, to help him, with Mme Wolff, to cross into Spain. As he was a Jew, he was scared of racial persecution. I agreed. And once we were up there, in the mountains, I told him how I felt. We argued. He threatened me with his stick. He hit me over the head. I fired my gun. His wife went for me. I fired again. It was legitimate self defence. As for the money, I didn't touch it. Despite the fact that, at the start, he had only paid me half the fee...

This simplistic explanation certainly does not receive the support of the court. The members of the jury are unmoved. There is a murmur from the public. As far as the murder of Edward Fleck is concerned, whose body has recently been discovered, Louis Martin's defence is even weaker:

'I went with him to the end of the track and then he told me he preferred to go on alone. We were close to the border. He knew the area well. I let him go. Probably robbers attacked him further on...

'Robbers, said the presiding judge, who, by coincidence, had a revolver of the same calibre as yours!

'Why not? cries M Houssepard. On the pretext that my client has, in a moment of exasperation, struck down two people who were threatening him, you cannot hold him responsible for every crime committed in the Hautes-Pyrenees during the German occupation.

This protest sparks off a battle of words between the defence and the prosecuting counsel. Voices are raised, time moves on. The presiding judge of Saulieu consults his advisors and declares that the court will rise and adjourn until the afternoon when the witnesses will be heard.

Etienne sighed with relief, as if he would benefit, at the same time as his father, from this brief remission. "What is he doing at the moment? They take him away, between two guards. They give him something to eat. But he is not hungry. His head feels heavy. He has trouble keeping his eyes open. The lawyer visits him, encourages him. Then they come to fetch him. And everything begins again. In the same room. In front of the same faces." The following day's newspaper. On the front page, this headline: *In the witness box, the murderer's second wife sobs.* The girl had finished reading. She re-powdered her face, got up, left her place, Etienne followed her with his eyes.

'No, your honour, my husband was not a wicked man. I married him in Cauterets in 1941, shortly after his divorce. He never spoke to me about his past life. I was happy with him. I managed the restaurant. He looked after the cinema. We had three showings each week...

Mme Louis Martin, née Catherine Raymonde Vivien, is seen to be a tall, thin, blond woman with sharp features and sad eyes. Her voice shakes with emotion. While she is speaking, the accused leans sadly towards her. Several times she looks at him, her eyes full of pity. The presiding judge of Saulieu asks:

'How could it happen that, living on perfectly good terms with your husband, you were in no way suspicious of his actions? You could not have been unaware of his nocturnal expeditions! What explanation did he give you?

'He used to tell me that he was in the Resistance, that he was helping patriots cross the border. I was afraid for him. I used to advise him to be careful...

'Delightful consideration! says the counsel for the prosecution.

'And when he would come back, how did you find him? asks the presiding judge.

Mme Martin becomes flustered. Her shoulders quiver with a sudden sob. She groans:

'I don't know, he would seem tired and happy. He would laugh at nothing. He would make fun of the Germans because he had thwarted their tricks.

The counsel for the prosecution, wearing his red gown, stands:

'I am asking members of the jury to remember every word of this vital testimony. So, the accused would not feel the least remorse following his crimes. After soaking his hands in the blood...

The room was gradually emptying. Soon the bell for closing time would ring. Etienne was afraid that he would not have enough time to finish the article he was reading. He skipped a few lines.

'Have the next witness enter.

The elderly gentleman closed the book he was reading, got up, blew his nose, looked into his handkerchief.

'Goodbye, he said

'Goodbye, said Etienne.

'Will you turn to the members of the jury and reply.

At the witness box there now stands a smart young woman in a black suit. Her face is so delicate and pale that it could be modelled in wax. She is the first Mme Martin, nee Marie-Louis Loiselet.

Etienne stared straight ahead: "She never told me that. She was there. As a witness. In front of all these people. Oh! That's dreadful!" Tears stung the roof of his mouth. He wanted to push back his chair, to run away.

'You lived with the accused from 1931 to 1939. You had a son by him. Will you tell us if Louis Martin's behaviour led you to predict the crimes which have been referred to the court?

The former Mme Martin gives her husband a transparent glance. She seems very sure of herself. Not at all upset. She says:

'I do not believe so, your Honour. My husband was certainly a person of unstable temperament. Sometimes gentle and sometimes brutal. His mood would change for no apparent reason. We often argued. I used to reproach him especially for his laziness, his infidelities. But those are grievances of a secondary nature.

'What was the reason for your divorce?

'My husband deserted the family home, leaving me alone and

without the means of supporting my child.

'Did he attempt to meet up with you after your separation?

'No.

'Did he try to see his son?

'Again, no.

'So, did he have no affection for him?

'I do not know, your Honour...

Etienne had the impression that a thousand pairs of eyes were turned towards him, fixing him to his chair. He was suddenly, and in a categorical, undeniable way, the son of Louis Martin. He felt completely dirty inside, in his head, his mouth, his stomach. A flow of shame, like mud, yellow and sickly, was lapping under his skin.

'What I would like to know from the witness, says the counsel for the prosecution, is if she was surprised to learn, from the newspapers, that her ex-husband had been arrested on the charge of deliberate homicide.

The young woman seems flustered by this insidious question. She turns her face away. Her hands tighten on the edge of the witness box.

"Poor Marion. She is suffering. She is struggling. She does not know what to say. And I am far away. I cannot help her."

'Yes, it seems incredible, your Honour.

"How kindly she is towards him, despite all she has suffered because of him! Please don't cry!" An exclamation rose into Etienne's throat and stopped on his lips: "Mum!"

Nobody had heard him. People carried on reading, thinking, breathing in ignorance.

The presiding judge of Saulieu questions the witness again about the morality of the accused, his annual income, his expenditure, the company he kept.

'We are closing.

Etienne jumped and looked up. Brought face to face with the stark demands of reality, he took some time again to recognise the place and time which were imposing themselves on him. A kindly library attendant indicated the clock, the room now half empty.

'A few minutes more, he stammered, I haven't finished.

'Come back tomorrow. We can keep the volume for you. You will only have to fill in a pink form at the desk.

'That's right...Yes...Keep the volume for me, said Etienne.

He left the room in a complete daze, his legs weak, alarmed to the depths of his being. The idea of seeing Marion again, after what he had read, terrified him. He wondered if he would have enough energy to pretend that he had spent the afternoon with Palaiseau. "I must. For her and for me. If not, all is lost." He descended some steps, crossed the entrance hall of the Library and hurried towards the main exit.

'Martin!

The shout rolled like a clap of thunder and echoed in the corridors, in the empty rooms. Etienne, taken by surprise, thought he was dreaming. He turned round. In front of him stood M Thuillier, his philosophy teacher. The big man, huddled behind his gold framed glasses and his black leather wallet, was smiling, nodding his head and saying:

'I'm blowed if I expected to meet you here Martin!...

Etienne experienced the absurd feeling of being unmasked, betrayed, arrested. Every vein in his body quivered. He murmured:

'I was in the periodicals room...I was reading. You haven't gone away for the holidays?..

'No, said M Thuillier. I preferred to stay in Paris to finish my book. It seemed to Etienne as if M Thuiller's eyes were piercing his head as a knife cuts through butter. "Do I look as if I have read what I have read? Is it obvious that I am the son of a murderer? Is it written on my face?" M Thuillier held out his hand:

'Goodbye, Martin.

'Goodbye.

They went their separate ways.

Chapter Five

❛We had been walking for more than three hours, on mule tracks, steep and rocky. The night was cool and silent. In front of me I saw Louis Martin's back swaying from side to side...

The man who is speaking is none other than Gerard Methivier, a chemical engineer, aged 37, of Bordeaux. who was able, miraculously, to avoid being killed. He is a well built lad, with a tanned complexion, with lavender blue eyes and sparkling teeth. In 1943, after the Gestapo had searched his home, he had resolved to flee in order to join up with the Free French Forces. Two friends, who had since died after being deported, gave him Louis Martin's address.

'What was the accused's behaviour like towards you during the first part of your expedition? asks the presiding judge.

'He showed himself to be very warm towards me and confirmed that I was running no risk in following the route that he had established. On two occasions he made me stop and sit down on a rock, as he wanted to massage my right ankle which was painful because of a sprain...

At these words, an indignant murmur ran through the public gallery. The counsel for the prosecution cried:

'Members of the jury will take note!

The defence barrister turned towards the accused and spoke softly to him.

'At about two o'clock in the morning, continues the witness, we reached a small pine wood on a rocky hill side. "Is the border still a long way off", I asked. He smiled and answered, shaking his head: " About an hour's walk." Then he handed me a flask and invited me to drink a mouthful of rum to keep my strength up. I admit that I was touched by so much concern. "You deserve better than the job you are doing, I told him. A good Frenchman like you shouldn't be getting paid to help patriots flee German persecution." He gave me a nasty look and replied: "Why do you say that? Because you do not want to pay me the second half of the amount?" I began laughing: "You will have the money, don't worry. " At that exact moment – God knows why – I felt apprehensive deep down. I couldn't make out my guide's face in the darkness. Yet, it seemed that his eyes were widening, advancing towards me, staring, luminous, like the eyes of an animal. My hand held the flask. I raised the top to my lips. Suddenly a shot from a gun rang out. Then another. I had the impression that it wasn't a bullet that was striking my face, but an iron bar, a hammer, thrown at point blank range. I rolled down the slope, falling about three metres. Through a confused buzzing. I heard Louis Martin swearing: "Bastard! Bastard!" His heavy footstep grated against the pebbles. I thought I was finished. But, suddenly, everything changed. His footsteps were disappearing into the distance. There was a crack of branches. I fainted.

When I opened my eyes again, a man I did not know was leaning over me and washing my face with a cloth soaked in water. He was a woodcutter. His arrival on the scene had disturbed Louis Martin, who had thought it better to run off. The good man spoke hardly any French. He took me back to his hut. Fortunately, only one bullet had hit me. Even better, it had only gashed my cheek. The following day, I crossed the border. Three days later I was arrested and imprisoned by the Spanish authorities. I passed myself off as a Canadian paratrooper. The Canadian consul was willing to support my story. In January 1944 I was in London.

The witness stops speaking and lowers his eyes. A dismayed silence hangs over the court. In the dock Louis Martin himself seems appalled, as if he has seen a ghost with an expression bent on revenge.

'In the light of what they have just heard, declares the prosecuting counsel, members of the jury will imagine the suffering of those who did not have Gerard Metivier's good fortune.

'M Martin, asks the presiding judge, do you acknowledge the accuracy of the facts which have been recounted to you?

'Yes, says Louis Martin. But this man seemed to me to be suspect. He was speaking with too much kindness. It was strange the way he was waiting at the place where we had stopped. I figured that he was perhaps a Gestapo agent and that he had led me there so that I would be caught red handed by a German patrol. When I heard footsteps behind me, I lost my head, I fired a shot, and ran off.

Etienne turned the page, After what he had read, he felt that no revelation could surprise him. A calm horror had taken root in his soul. Once again, he congratulated himself on having been able to maintain, in front of his mother, the day before, on returning home from the National Library, an everyday expression. This test of will finished in his favour. The testimony of witnesses called by the defence was of no interest at all. The discussion around the exhibits in the case, displayed on the table at the back of the court, dragged on and on. A newspaper photograph showed a revolver, a piece of rope, a knife, a cloth stained with black blood.

'Members of the jury, says the counsel for the prosecution, the individual you have in front of you...

Etienne's neighbour, a young man, his forehead covered with small yellow spots, got up, consulted the catalogue, returned to his place.

'Presently, they shall try to present the accused as an irresponsible person, who, at the drop of a hat, would lose control of his actions. For my part, I maintain that Louis Martin is a deliberate and wily killer, a murderer of the vilest sort and that the acceptance in his favour, of the slightest attenuating circumstance, would amount to an insult to the memory of his victims. Let us take the facts one by one...

Etienne read the summary of the indictment attentively. From time to time, a sentence would catch his attention, would cause him to flush:

The murderer's intimate life... The despicable calculations of the man who, already, is generally known as "the monster of Cauterets"...

The spotty young man dropped his pen and bent down to pick it up. Instinctively, Etienne half closed the book. "He mustn't see what I am reading. He might suspect something." His temples were buzzing, as if his head had got stuck under a bell. All the muscles of his face were hurting. "I am a different type of person. They cannot understand me." The young man sat up again and went back to his reading. "Quickly, quickly, where was I?"

Louis Martin is only a shadow of his former self. Clearly, the prosecution counsel's words are removing any hope of saving his skin. Pale, fascinated, he is reliving, hour by hour, the successive dramas of which he was the sad and principal protagonist. It is to M Houssepard that falls the thankless task of reconciling the members of the jury to the human scarecrow, who finds himself at the mercy of their decision. He fulfils his mission with rare eloquence and skill. Refuting point by point the theft argument, he retains against Louis Martin only the accusation of the murder of M and Mme Leon Wolff and the attempted murder of M Gerard Metivier. Then, referring again to the statements of the witnesses, he contrives to prove that they are in agreement in presenting the accused as a strange type of man, a man of changeable moods, capable in turns of the most delicate concern and the worst excesses. In short, according to him, Louis Martin is suffering from a specific type of insanity and his case should be a matter for psychiatry rather than for justice.

'Members of the jury, look at this man. I have studied him closely. He is lucid. He discusses, he reasons like you and me. But, suddenly, under the influence of an internal shock, his whole being breaks down. His moral values collapse. A wave of blood invades his brain. This attack of violence overtook him frequently in the open countryside, at high altitude, as if the open space, the night, the silence had provoked in him the need to kill. Believe me, Louis Martin's victims were not chosen by him. They found themselves there at the moment of his crisis. Despite the evidence, the examining judge has refused to allow a mental examination of my client to take place. However, I am in a position to deliver to the court documents from the doctor treating Louis Martin. From these documents, it transpires that Louis Martin is well and truly a person with excessive, unforeseeable reactions...

Etienne placed his hands on his thighs, as if to prevent himself from hitting someone. Thoughts running to and fro were dislocating his mind. By turns, his father was coming towards him and moving away from him. "A mad man? A murderer? How could one know?"

Accepting M Houssepard's request, the court postpones the continuation of the case until the following day, and specifies a doctor, who, meanwhile, will examine Louis Martin and give his verbal report to the court.

A night in a cell, a night of waiting, hoping, of solitary fears. Etienne leafed through the book with its long, narrow pages, black with print, which fell softly to the left.

The war against Japan...might Hitler be alive...? Churchill, Stalin, General de Gaulle.

Finally, in capital letters, this black headline, vulgar, excessive: *Louis Martin will pay...* A photograph, "Good heavens, it's him! Standing up, his back hunched, his face dead. A face made of paper. And his eyes are looking down, as through holes cut in a mask."

The specialist's report commissioned by the court formally concludes that Louis Martin is entirely responsible; he is not considered as being in a state of insanity in the sense of article 64 of the penal code. The accused is led away. Members of the jury retire to deliberate. After a quarter of an hour they return to the court. The presiding judge reads out the replies to the questions asked and, in a grave voice, pronounces the verdict: it is the death sentence.

Etienne shuddered, as if he had just learned of this condemnation, at the same time as his father. The hairs were standing up on his flesh. "What? It's not possible..."

Louis Martin stands up. The guards lead him away. The presiding judge of Saulieu puts his cap back on his head. The court empties. This is a sentence of the court which is not likely to be disputed.

Another wad of useless pages. Then, dated 14th June, these few lines in small print:

The appeal for mercy for Louis Martin having been rejected, the murderer was led from his prison yesterday morning, at dawn, to be taken to his place of execution...

"My father is walking between two policemen. The coolness of the early morning on his face, on his neck. The last bursts of fresh air, of sounds, of colours, of scents. Suddenly, right in front of him, the vertical silhouette of the guillotine. He steps back. He resists. He wants to stay there, among men, among us, living. A priest speaks to him. No doubt there are inquisitive people standing around. People with filthy, greedy faces. Boars, pigs, snakes. Somebody pushes him in the back. He falls forward. The blade whistles. His head rolls into a basket of bran. A flow of blood gushes forth red, quick." Etienne received the flow of blood full in the face. He was shivering. His teeth were chattering. A dismal taste, sickening, was filling his mouth. He looked around him. The spotty young man was reading a travel article. A golden light suffused all these profiles leaning forward, all these open books, all these studious hands. "Decent people killed my father." He passed his tongue over his lips. His finger was leafing through the volume backwards. Subconsciously, he was returning to the time when Louis Martin was still alive. The photo of the guilty man. It was in the last column. A mad idea crossed Etienne's mind. "Cut it out. It's not allowed. But it is allowed for me. I am his son." He took a penknife from his pocket, opened it under the table, surreptitiously. "And if they see me? If they stop me? They will ask me my name. The library pass. Impossible to deny. The murderer's son cuts a photo of his father out of the newspaper. A fine scandal in prospect. The headlines in the daily papers. My mother in tears.. No, I can't..."

Quite motionless, he was suffering, at the same time, attacks of temptation and of fear. The grey and white photo fascinated him, attracted him, as if it were shining at the end of a long corridor. He was walking towards it. He was obeying the command of these eyes, unhappy and terrible, which had stopped living. "I must do it. Not for me, for him. It is he who is begging me to take it, to get it out of there. The blade of the knife slipped over the page. Etienne gripped the edge of the page between two fingers. A tearing noise resounded deep in his bones. It was the crack of a glacier opening in the middle. Everyone had heard it. Everyone had seen it. He swallowed back a mouthful of saliva and cast a fearful look at his neighbours. Their peaceful demeanour reassured him. The idiots! To create a diversion, he crumpled a few sheets of the scrap paper which were lying in front of him on the table. Then, with deliberation, he stuffed the photograph into his jacket pocket and closed the volume. Finished. He had won. He could withdraw, his head held high.

*

'There you are at last, my darling! cried Marion. I was waiting for you. I might need you...

She was sitting in front of the dining room table and was attaching epaulettes to a dress. Mme Marthe, leaning over her sewing machine, in the crouching attitude of a cycle racer, was pedalling furiously without looking up. This considerable disorder created an atmosphere of female work, tense and petty. Marion pushed the sewing thimble further onto her finger, stuck the needle into the fabric and spoke again:

'Would you believe that Mlle Suzanne hasn't come in this afternoon. A bad bout of 'flu. She is off for six days at least. And all this work waiting!

'It's certainly very annoying, said Etienne, making an effort.

'Do you want me to speak to my caretaker's daughter? said Mme Marthe. She does a bit of dressmaking. Perhaps she will agree to come as a replacement.

'It won't be the same, said Marion.

'No, of course not. But she will always be able to help us with the easy jobs.

Etienne was looking at these faces, listening to these voices from another world. An abyss separated him from his mother, a river, a lake of blood.

'Listen, Etienne, You can do me a favour. Daisy is waiting for her dress for dinner. We ought to get it to her straightaway. You can take a taxi...

'Yes, mum..

She cut the thread, got up, took a piece of paper from the sideboard.

'Leave that, I'll do the parcel, said Mme Marthe.

While Mme Marthe was wrapping the dress, Marion was writing the address on the back of a visiting card:

'Don't stop at the caretaker's room. Go straight up to Daisy's flat. She's expecting you.

Mme Marthe gave Etienne a soft, flexible parcel, secured by pins. Carrying this burden, he felt suddenly mystified, made to look ridiculous, diverted from his true objective. "On my arm Daisy's dress, in my pocket the photo of my father, put to death by the guillotine. Am I dreaming?" He hovered from one leg to the other, indecisive, angry. Marion looked at him anxiously, with an insistence which he found difficult to endure. Then she pushed him towards the door, murmuring:

'Off you go, quickly, darling, it's important.

Chapter Six

He put his bedside lamp back on, sat down and listened to the silence of the house, which was drifting, like a steamship, in the night. Seven floors of dreams, of closed eyelids, of parallel breathing. In this vessel of silent stones, Etienne was alone in not being able to sleep. In vain, for two hours, had he tried to forget his anguish. The trial was playing out in his mind for the hundredth time. Through the words of the presiding judge, the counsel for the prosecution, the barrister, the witnesses, the accused, he was trying to reconstitute the drama and to draw up his own judgement.

One fact seemed to him undeniable: contrary to the accusations of the prosecution, Louis Martin had not killed in order to take possession of the victims' money, but in obedience to the demands of a criminal obsession. Without being insane, as his defending counsel maintained, he displayed the characteristics of a vindictive man, easily angered and morose. The violence and the absurdity, even, of his actions excluded every idea of calculation. "So what? He killed. And, because of him, Marion has known days of loneliness and humiliation. Because of him, I shall never again be able to live the same life as other people. Because of him, everything is different, rotten, poisoned, in the world which surrounds me."

He got out of bed and stepped onto the coarse, worn out rug. A floor tile creaked. "Marion must not hear". Stepping lightly, he went over to the table. For a long while he had struggled against the desire to see the photograph again. But the temptation was too great. When he had seen the picture, everything would be better. His chest was burning under his pyjama jacket. Through the partly open shutters the dark, warm breath of the city entered the room. He sat on a chair, opened the drawer. The relics were there, placed side by side, as in a shop window. With obsessive care, he took them out, one after another, and placed them on a piece of blotting paper. The scrap of newspaper was folded into four. Etienne smoothed it out with the flat of his hand. Contrary to expectation, no emotion at all was engendered in him by this document, which he knew in minute detail. He thought for a moment that he had made a mistake, that he was examining the portrait of someone else. Studying the mother of pearl cuff links and the pig skin wallet in no way changed his indifference.

Around the bedroom, which the bedside lamp lit in an oblique, dramatic manner, the shadows had no effect on him. Disappointed, Etienne pushed away the cuff links and the wallet, and directed his eyes to the watch: a very ordinary watch, with a gilded metal case, a round glass, a tarnished strap. The face, pale yellow in colour, was dirty with dust. The hands had stopped at twenty past twelve. Etienne took the watch, weighed it in his hands, wound it up. And suddenly, as if by magic, it responded with a regular ticktock. He was so surprised that his hands began to tremble. Louis Martin was dead, but his watch carried on living. With a brisk movement Etienne put it back on the blotting paper. Something rebelled deep within him against this stupid mechanism which persisted in measuring time, despite the fact that time had ceased to exist for its owner. The ticking of the watch was becoming deafening, was filling the bedroom, was regulating the life of the whole house.

Someone was coming. It was certain. A robot's step was entering the passage. "Who is it? A shoulder strikes the door. It shatters in pieces. And he comes in. Him. My father." A commotion ran through Etienne's nerves and gave him a parched, burning taste at the back of his mouth. "And if it were true? How would I welcome him? Would I be for or against him? Would I recognise him by his face alone?"

Etienne had never seen corpses. He was imagining rows of worthy dead people, washed, shaved, with combed hair, with smooth cheeks and with a dignified look in the recesses of their eyes. Respectful hands had taken care to dress these ceremonial models. They had knotted their smart ties. They had polished their shoes. They had placed flowers and candles around their bodies lying in rest. Louis Martin did not belong to this worthy race. "All dead people have a head. Mine does not. He has had his neck sliced. He has been buried in two pieces. Where?" He realised with amazement that he did not know where the tomb was. Why look for it? Louis Martin had probably been buried in a common grave. "Anyway, that doesn't change anything. Worms do not distinguish between the honest civil servant and the poor bloke who has been guillotined. They like all flesh. The judge who condemned my father will rot in the same way as him. They will become part of the same earth. They will feed the same vegetation. It is men who invent moral differences, who award honours, who apportion blame, print money and operate the guillotine. I had the prize for all round excellence and my father is a murderer. If they had known that my father was a murderer, would they have given me the prize for all round excellence?"

He had stood up and was walking, up and down, in the bedroom. His shadow, larger than life, broke on the ceiling mouldings. From time to time the wardrobe mirror reflected the image of limp, striped pyjamas above which blazed the face of an exterminating angel. For the moment, in order to reinforce his conviction, Etienne called to his aid the memories of a father's glance, of a friendly smile, a heavy hand clumsily caressing his hair. His father holding him in his arms, in front of a brightly lit shop window. His father filling his pipe, reading a newspaper, cutting the bread. His father leaning over his bed to kiss him.

"Yes, but he leaned in the same way over a human being he had just struck down. The hollow, empty night, with its silent rocks, its twinkling stars. On the ground a body twisted in an awkward pose, its legs askew, its arms crossed, its chin firm. A few seconds before, this body had a life, a soul, relatives, friends, obligations, a blister on its foot, heartburn, identity papers, an aim in life, a vocation, a homeland. One bullet from a revolver had been enough to empty the envelope, to deflate the balloon. There is no longer anything of interest under this skin, which is going cold. With both hands, Louis Martin spreads out the clothes, rummages in the pockets. Beneath his fingers this sacrificed flesh, this dampness of blood. In his nostrils, the smell of the nothingness which is coming into being. He pulls out a wallet stuffed with banknotes. Perhaps that very one which I keep in my table drawer? Oh! It would be awful. No, he didn't steal. I am sure he didn't steal. And the watch? And the cuff links?"

Etienne glanced at the objects, as if their appearance alone would have been enough to give him the information. "To whom do you belong? Where do you come from?" The surface of the objects could not be penetrated. "He pushes the body into a hole. He rolls a torrent of loose stones over it. He stands up again. He is alone. No-one has seen him. But *I* have seen him."

This idea strikes him like a blow from an axe. He reels. The plaster bust, with its black eyes and hair, was beginning to think in a confused, clumsy, lifeless way. Signs of colour were coming to life in the mottled wings of the butterflies. The walls were moving. "I have seen him and I shall denounce him. He deserves it. But if I denounce him, he will be arrested, interrogated and killed."

He sat down again at the table and held his head in his hands. The silence of the night imprisoned him in pool of oil. When he thought about Louis Martin's death, he hated the men who had judged him, and, when he thought about the victims' deaths, he recognised that Louis Martin deserved his condemnation. Drawn between the horror of what his father had done and the horror of what they had done to his father, he was becoming the centre of an endless debate. On the table the watch ticked away unperturbed. "The fact that he is my father is not an extenuating circumstance. Besides he never took any interest in me. I hardly remember him. I scarcely love him. And if I were suddenly to learn that I am not his son?" He shuddered and stood up again. The plaster bust looked at him with a degree of interest.

"Marion comes back in tears and admits her fault: I am not the son of Louis Martin, but of Pierre Dupont, or Roger Duval. Everything is changed. I am saved. I escape, light and graceful, from the glue where, already, my paws were becoming stuck." He tried to live, in advance, this minute of marvellous relief. Delivered from his obsession, he was resuming his former existence, comfortable, exemplary, hard working. Books, friends, mum, exams. "No, I would no longer be able to. I have been marked. If not by blood, at least by name. Whatever happens, I shall be on the side of the headless man. I shall not leave him on his own to be the butt of everybody's scorn. Anyway, what is the point of discussion? I am his son. I know it. I feel it." A wave of pride fills his breast: "They are all against him. I am alone in daring to defend him. He killed, at night, led by an evil compulsion. Others executed him in cold blood, deliberately, in broad daylight, applying the law and by virtue of powers which had been conferred upon them. Therefore, they are more guilty than he. Killers of a killer. Murderers to the power of two. Judges, executioners, witnesses, victims are soaked in the same blood. Error and truth, justice and crime are intertwined. And on this muddled dung heap grow the flowers of Christian thought."

In the confusion which was disturbing him, he would like to have been succoured, convinced by some decisive speech. But where, with whom, could he find comfort? The philosophers themselves did not agree on the concept of punishment. Pure theological dogma, Kantian ethics, eudemonism[1], utilitarian ethics, evolutionary ethics. From Thomas Aquinas[2] to Plato[3], to Kant[4], to Schopenhauer, to Spencer[5] to Guyau[6], to Bergson[7], each was saying his piece, and yet the world was continuing to turn in space, with its sun, its moon, its cities, its mountains, its magistrates and its criminals.

What certainty could there be in moral principles, given that the principles of physics changed from one generation to another? How was it that notions of Good and Evil should be immutable for courts of law, whereas the notion of energy, for example, varied from century to century and from expert to expert. By what right could judges affirm that one person was guilty and another innocent, seeing that they did not know, seeing that they could never know, the truth about the body and soul of the one who was awaiting the sentence?

M Thuillier had devoted a special lesson to the concept of justice and particularly to the death penalty. The school books were arranged in a pile under the table. Etienne kneeled down, demolished the structure and pulled towards him an exercise book with a dark brown cover: *Lessons on Morality*. The writing of a well behaved schoolboy. Headings underlined with a red pencil. "I still wasn't Louis Martin's son. I was only Marion's son." He leafed quickly through this wad of handwritten pages.

> Considered objectively, and from the most basic standpoint, the death penalty is a means of defence which society has against those who threaten to destroy its structure. However, if we pass from the social point of view to the individual one...

This writing annoyed him. He threw the exercise book onto the table, went over to the window, pushed open the iron shutters. A pure and lukewarm night spread out over the roofs of the city. Tiny stars shone in the limited area of blue space which he could see. From the sky to the earth there came down advice to be accepted without question: "This is the truth. What am I in relation to these stars? In what way is my destiny more interesting than the destiny of a gnat? The same stars were glittering in the firmament when my father was walking in the mountains. It was beneath their indifferent gaze that he murdered. No human gesture could disturb the fundamental harmony of nature."

He closed the shutters, threw himself down on the bed, put out the light. Now that the room was in darkness again, the ticktock of the watch was increasing in strength and precision. Etienne lay on his stomach and buried his head in the pillow. Then, it seemed that someone was standing behind him and raising an arm like a statue. With a start, he turned round. Nothing. Emptiness. Darkness. The house which is digesting, breathing, snoring. For a long while Etienne remained in that position, his back stiff, his neck tense, his eyes fixed on the darkness of the room. His muscles were going numb. Ideas were going round and round in his head. He went to sleep only when dawn was breaking.

Chapter Seven

It was Marion who woke him up by knocking on the door:

'Get up, Etienne, your friend is here.

His head leaden. his eyelids stuck, he was still struggling to free himself from the end of a dream:

'Which friend?

'Bernard Palaiseau.

He turned over in his bed:

'I don't want to see him.

'You can't say that, Etienne. I told him I was going to call you. He's waiting in the hall.

He groaned:

'What's the time, then?

'Eleven o'clock. I've had breakfast without you. If you want your coffee...

'No point.

'Yesterday you must have read very late in bed.

'Yes, mum.

'It's madness!

She went off. Etienne got up, put on a dressing gown, combed his hair with the palm of his hand and opened the door:

'Come in here, Bernard, it's quieter.

The boy came lolloping into the room:

'I'm not disturbing you? I was passing by on my bike...

Etienne was looking with embarrassment at this little person, carefree and well washed, wearing yellow shoes. Was it possible that, less than a week before, Bernard Palaiseau had been for him an acceptable companion?

'We've still got time to go for a ride in the Bois, declared Bernard Palaiseau.

'I don't fancy it, murmured Etienne. I can't be bothered.

He turned his back on his friend and pretended to tidy some books

64

on his table. Now he could not tolerate Bernard Palaiseu's presence in his bedroom. What was he doing, coming into his house, this red haired wishy-washy character, with his nonsense about bike rides, Sunday billiards and silly girls? With one bound, Etienne had escaped this kingdom of childhood. He no longer had anything in common with young blokes of his age. His secret isolated him, raised him above them, rendered him incomprehensible, unapproachable. "What could I say to him? What interests him does not interest me. We no longer have the same reasons for living, and we no longer speak the same language."

'What about this afternoon, asked Bernard Palaiseau, are you free?

'No, said Etienne.

'Pity, replied Bernard. Biosque and Maroussel have got back from their holidays. We're going to have a drink , together, in a little cafe in the Latin Quarter: *Le Fisto*. I was there yesterday. It's a real laugh. We saw Thuillier. He said hello...

'I'm sorry, said Etienne.

Under the skin of his neck, his arms and his thighs, his nerves, too tense, were becoming painful. "How far removed I am from him! how I am to be pitied! What's going to become of me?"

'You really ought to come with us. There will be two girls there, who Maroussel picked up on holiday in La Baule...

'I can't, said Etienne. I promised my mother I would go out with her.

Palaiseau gave him a sharp look:

'If you're fed up with me pestering you like this just say so, he said.

'Of course not, Bernard. Only, I'm very busy at the moment. That's all. Later, we'll see...

And he thought with horror, with intoxication: "If he knew! If he could understand!" Bernard Palaiseau placed his index finger on the nose of the plaster bust:

'Understood. I'm off. You'll be in touch.

'I promise, said Etienne.

At lunchtime, Marion asked him if he was meeting up, in the afternoon, with his friend.

'No, said Etienne. He's too stupid. I prefer to be on my own..

'That's a pity, my darling, she said. You must get out, enjoy yourself. I don't like to see you with your nose in a book all day long...

Marion's worried tone of voice brought Etienne back into line. He had forgotten his role. In order not to alarm his mother, he had to maintain the exhausting pretence of serenity:

'Don't feel sorry for me, Marion. I am very well as I am. You know I love reading. It's my vice.

While speaking, he was forcing upon his face a smile, a joyful expression. And Marion so wanted to be reassured, that she was credulous in welcoming the slightest signs of this pretence of a good mood.

'You truly are a funny boy, Etienne...

'Perhaps, mum, but you must let me live in my own way. At the moment I have a fantastic plan.

'What is it?

'I would like...I would like to write a book, an essay on the events occurring in our dreams.

She opened wide her childlike eyes:

' What does that mean?

'Situations created while we are dreaming. The problem has not been properly studied. I have my ideas about it...

He was speaking quickly, in order to bemuse her, dazzle her and divert her from her suspicions. The ease with which he lied amazed even himself. It was as if a cast iron ball was weighing on his heart; he wanted to confess, to open up, to ask advice, and yet from his lips flowed an elegant and deceitful speech:

'In fact, it's because we are unable to wake ourselves up that our dreams seem absurd. When we open our eyes, we tear apart a web of images, we break the harmony which is there. If we could retain in our memory the perfect chain of events which have made up our dream, we would be in the presence of a fine work of art. Do you understand?

'Yes, my darling. It's very interesting.

'Yes – isn't it?

'He had to grit his teeth to contain the sob which was forming in his throat. On the walls the cockerels, fixed in the hollows of the plates, were looking at him, judging him, coldly. "You are lying. You are the son of a murderer and you are lying."

'Suzanne is returning to work tomorrow, said Marion. It's a relief for me. I was shattered...

'How about Daisy, he asked, is she happy with her dress?

'Delighted. But she would like to have the pleats on the bodice removed. I feel it would be a mistake.

'Yes.

'She told me on the telephone this morning, that she found you a very handsome young man.

He assumed a hollow smile, stupidly, his mouth drawn, his cheeks stiff. Marion pointed at him forcefully:

'I don't think you find her unattractive, either...

'Me! I've hardly looked at her..

'You've made a mistake, She is stunning.

'He stuck his finger nails into the palms of his hands. This was a trial that was too strong for him. "I must get used to this. This will be my life from now on. Pretending, lying, keeping everything to myself." At last, Marion cleared the table. Mme Marthe rang at the door. And Etienne, on the pretext of urgent work, shut himself in his bedroom.

During the following days he returned to the National Library, to consult other accounts of the trial. All the newspapers he was able to read through presented the murderer as someone who did not deserve a pardon. By virtue of reading them, Etienne had learned by heart certain passages of the cases for the prosecution and the defence. He would recite them in the evening, before going to sleep. And it seemed to him that he was, by turns, the prosecuting counsel and the lawyer for his father.

However, at home, life continued unchanged in its most minor rituals. The dressmakers sewed, Marion sold dresses. And M Maxime Joubert telephoned each day at half past ten in the morning. On Friday the sewing machine broke down and a specialist came to repair it, under the distrustful eye of Mme Marthe. On Saturday these ladies received a visit from a South American customer who ordered three items at once.

On Sunday, after lunch, Marion suggested to her son that he go with her to the cinema for the matinee performance. He wanted to refuse her, but he held back for fear of upsetting his mother. They leaned together over the newspaper, open at the cinema listings. Etienne's eyes ran along the columns. Most were gangster films. Advertisements, at the bottom of the page, showed men with narrow foreheads, armed with smoking pistols, women's faces contorted with fear, splashes of black blood around a taut hand. *Hired Assassin...The Third Man...Raw Deal... News Item...Portrait of a Murderer...*Etienne felt Marion's embarrassment, faced with this collection of violent titles. Clearly, she did not want to impose on her son a spectacle which risked awakening in him the memory of Louis Martin. She was even already regretting her idea. She was saying:

'I don't see anything particularly wonderful...

He felt so sorry for her, to the point of wanting to cry out: "Poor Marion! How painful this must be!"

In order to put her mind at rest, he pointed towards a harmless title:

'Let's go and see that.

'What?

'The Blue Lagoon. That must be nice. It takes place on a Pacific island...

She thanked him with a smile:

'Yes, yes...you're right...

They had to queue outside the cinema and could only find seats at the side near the screen. The cinema was full. A stifling heat weighed down on the heads of the audience. The air smelt of acid sweets and recycled sweat. Marion took Etienne's hand and asked him:

'You're not too bad?

'Not at all.

On the screen appeared coloured images, which showed the wild sea, a ship's bridge, children's faces, an island covered with palm trees and bordered by soapy foam. For a few minutes Etienne was interested in the plot which unfolded nicely enough. Then he started, as if someone had caught him in the very act of being entertained. His personal torment forbad the least concession to feeling at ease. However imaginative film makers were, it would have been impossible for them to conceive and depict an adventure stranger than his own. "Is it acceptable for my mother, after what she has lived through, to take pleasure in such trifles as these?" He looked at Marion's profile, leaning towards the lighted rectangle where speaking phantoms were facing each other. "She is going along with it. She is captivated. She is living on a desert island, eating coconuts and swimming in a tide of turquoise blue waves. I am abandoned by everyone..."

A naked, muscular man dived into the sea, looking for pearl oysters. His arms split the water, spread apart the ribbons of seaweed which spat forth silver bubbles. brushed against large, sponge covered rocks, whence escaped a shoal of fish shaped like spearheads. Suddenly, from the depths of the abyss, a flabby face surged up, swelled, divided up into agile tentacles. The black and pink arms of the octopus fastened onto its prey, tying its limbs, encircling its body, wrapping around its neck. Attacked by eight serpents with their slimy rings, the unfortunate fisherman struggled in vain to reach the surface. Suckers of living rubber embraced him, crushed him, drew him towards a greedy mouth. Etienne held his breath, as if this unwise swimmer had been none other than himself. His lungs were emptying, his blood was beating in his ears. Marion, fascinated by this scene of horror, had leaned forward, her lips half open in a childish pout. "And what about me? I who am suffocating, suffering next to her, has she already forgotten me?" A cloud of black ink invaded the screen. The octopus was killed. The swimmer, saved, panting, was recovering on the knees of his companion, whose breasts were adorned with flowers and seashells. The music was flowing, sugary and slow, like cough syrup. Marion said:

'It's impressive, isn't it?

He did not reply. His own particular octopus was still living. When the word: "End" appeared on the screen, Etienne wiped his forehead and sat back in his seat.

'Shall we go? he asked.

'You don't want to see the news?

'No.

'Well then, let's go. Anyway, I've arranged to meet Daisy at about six o'clock in the basement of "Rond-Point" Do you want to come?...

He blushed:

'Sorry. I prefer to go home.

'As you wish, but Daisy will be disappointed.

She was teasing him, but kindly. She was inviting him into the world of humdrum feelings. "How little she knows of me!" The crowd was pushing them in the back. An obscure and stubborn herd, with empty expressions, faded make up, sweaty detachable collars. After an interminable time at a virtual standstill, they were at last expelled into the fresh air and Etienne breathed.

'What a stupid film! she said. Apart from the scene with the octopus...

'Good special effects.

'Still, it has whiled away some time. I shall be back for dinner.

He watched her walking away, light, dancing, in the blue and powdery light which suffused the Champs-Elysees. Soon her silhouette melted into the creeping mass of pedestrians. Etienne turned round and made his way to the bus stop. Some twenty people, queuing in a line, were waiting. "It will be quicker on foot", thought Etienne.

He was walking quickly in the avenue Marceau. Faces, notices, the noise of hooters accompanied his meditation. This last experience was conclusive. He no longer found any pleasure in anything. He could no longer get on with anyone. The revelation that he had received put him in a false position with the entire universe. Bravely, he tried to imagine his future: Etienne at thirty, Etienne at forty with a wife and kids, a job, something of a belly...It was laughable. "I am not viable", he said to himself. This idea struck his brain, and he stopped abruptly in front of the window of a leather ware shop. Yes, that was it: he had been thrown into the journey of life just to play a brief and dazzling role. A small rocket, hanging in the air, which explodes, shines and disappears. A cry, a burst, a gesture of rejection. "The world has rejected my father, I reject the world."

He began walking again, flat footed, his arms hanging at his side. "Why not? That would be the best solution. I have distanced myself from the herd. I suffer from being a special case. Seeing that the test is beyond my strength, it is better to do away with this grief by doing away with myself. Marion will cry but she will have Maxime Joubert to comfort her. Newspapers will publish articles about me. But I shall not be there to read them. Darkness, silence, oblivion. I don't believe in God. Therefore I am free." He thought of the small revolver which Marion kept hidden in her bedside table. "It's all so simple. You just need genuinely to have the will. This evening, perhaps..."

At the place de l'Alma, he waited for the policeman on duty to allow the pedestrians to cross the street. "It's stupid. I could have thrown myself under the wheels of a car. No, at home, it's at home that I want to die." A little further on, he felt tired and sat down on a bench. Next to him a couple of old men, tidily dressed, were following, with dazed expressions, the continuous movement of the cars. The sight of these two people, lined, hunched, stuck one against the other like shipwreck survivors on a raft, filled him with a quiet revulsion. Death was preferable to such degeneration. Every man worthy of the name must renounce, in advance, the hideous defects of senility. "The warts, the white hair, the wrinkled skin, the bad smell, the smiling imbecility will not be for me. I am young. I want to remain young. And I can only remain young by killing myself." When he arrived in front of the house, his decision had been firmly taken. In his mind a wonderful peace had succeeded the mess of contradictory reflections. Between the walls of the huge, empty flat, his footsteps echoed with solemnity. The bedside table had been placed there simply to fulfil his desire. He opened the drawer. In the middle of a heap of aspirin tubes, odd buttons and business cards, the revolver, small and black, slumbered, awaiting its time. Etienne slipped the gun into the depths of his pocket and shut himself in his bedroom, closing the door with the double lock.

The bedroom became attentive, froze, accepted its role as a stage set. Etienne believed he was alone and yet a huge crowd was watching him. He found himself on a stage, raised up, facing the abyss where a sombre mass of spectators were crowding round. It was as in a bad dream. One must act out a play which one hasn't yet rehearsed. And suddenly the curtain goes up, the audience is there. One must act, speak. "But I don't know how to go about it. I haven't learned." He took out of the drawer the photograph of Louis Martin, the cufflinks, the wallet, the watch. The watch had stopped. He wound it up, set it to the right time and placed it in a prominent position on the table, with the other items.

The revolver was pulling on the lining of his pocket. He took it in his hand, gripped it tightly. A sensation of cool metal ran along his arm and lodged under his armpit. "Especially, don't take time to think, stick the barrel five centimetres from the ear, pull the trigger. And then? …" His muscles were soft. A terrible weight in the shape of a bean, weighed on his fingers. It seemed that the crowd was becoming impatient: "Quickly, quickly, get on with it!" He raised his hand. The small steel circle pressed against his temple. The wardrobe mirror reflected back the image of a young man, blond and pale, in the process of making a telephone call. It was ridiculous. He turned his back on the mirror. "Let's get it over with." If someone had agreed to pull the trigger instead of him, he would have been able to die without killing himself! Impossible. Etienne had to do it all himself. "My father was more fortunate. They dragged him towards the guillotine. He had only to obey."

At the present time, the objects, the walls, previously insensitive, were joining forces against him, exuding vile eulogies, oozing sickly sweet reminiscences, causing the insidious memory of sleeplessness, of lime blossom tea, of blotting paper, of rice soup, of school books and of lead soldiers to float in the air. The essence of his past encircled him, imprisoned him and delayed his decision. He had to resolve to destroy not only this moment of his life, but his entire life, which was flowing in waves behind him, around him, like the tail of an exotic fish. The thought of everything that was going to stop living, as soon as he had stopped living himself, froze his bones with a solemn dread. The watch was nibbling something with small rat's teeth. "One, two, three...at twenty seven I shall kill myself...No: at thirty...I've plenty of time."

He would like to have taken into death the objects, the people he liked: Marion, his bicycle, some books, the photograph. But it was not allowed. Everything had to be left behind on the bank. Clothes and memories, with a label attached. A chasm blew into his face its breath of damp earth. That's what it was, nothingness. He was leaning over nothingness. He was entering nothingness, by small jolts. "Courage. One click. The act of scoring a point at billiards. And the problem will be resolved." Rumblings ran through the crowd. "What is he waiting for? It's ludicrous. He cannot do without men, nor live among them." Etienne's finger pressed weakly on the trigger. And, immediately, it seemed that a bullet was piercing the bones of his skull, was bursting into his brain with clots of blood, with splatters of bone marrow, with flames of pain.

He was reeling, turning in the wind, collapsing onto the ground and melting into the floor. "Idiot! Why did I do that? Now, it's too late." In the wardrobe mirror the young man was still standing and holding a revolver in his hand. Etienne sighed with relief: "I didn't shoot." His knees began to tremble. It was as if he were collapsing limply into himself. His whole body was breaking down. He no longer desired anything. He was afraid. Afraid of death and afraid of life. The audience was booing him, whistling in disapproval. A second time, without conviction, he brought the revolver close to his temple. But now he knew that the posture was not dangerous. "This is what people do when they want to kill themselves. But I do not want to kill myself. I shall not kill myself." His eyes swelled with a flood of tears: "Marion...Marion...Help!.." The revolver fell on the table. Etienne leaned back against the wall, his arms hanging at his sides, his head lowered, as at the end of a merciless fight. He was panting: "I must find someone to talk to...Otherwise I shall go mad...Already I no longer know who I am!" A passionate desire seized him to flee from this motionless room, to plunge into the light, into the noise, to be seen and heard by people with faces of flesh. He opened the door, rushed onto the landing, hurtled down the first steps of the staircase. Then he stopped, thought: "Damn! The revolver. I haven't put it back in its place. He retraced his steps, picked up the gun and replaced it in Marion's bedside table. He could feel his heart beating even in his toes. His feeling of self disgust was so strong that he promised himself that he would find another opportunity to die.

Chapter Eight

'Do come in! said M Thuillier.

'I wouldn't want to inconvenience you...

'What a thought! I had finished working! I live alone! And I'm not expecting anyone! In other words, you arrive at just the right time...

Etienne went into a small room, low and dirty, which seemed to him to have been cut out from shoddy cardboard. A desk lamp, covered with a yellowish green shade, cast a glow, as if underwater, on reefs of books half collapsing and slabs of white paper. The air was saturated with a heavy smell of tobacco. A wide plank, placed on trestles, served as a table.

'Take a seat, said M Thuillier pointing to a cane armchair.

He remained standing, his hands in his pockets, his belly prominent. He was in shirtsleeves, his tie knotted low down. Two gold frames outlined the bulging lenses of his glasses. A cigarette end, no longer alight, hung from his lip. Etienne was finding it difficult to breathe. Deep within him, beneath heavy layers of inert flesh, he felt his heart beating. A feeling of dizziness rose in him from the floor, which was bare and dirty with cinders. "I'm going to be sick", thought Etienne.

'Do you have any news? asked M Thuillier.

Etienne leaned forward a little. The armchair creaked. 'I need you, sir, said Etienne with a controlled voice.

'M Thuillier continued looking at him:

'Oh! really?

'Yes...I must tell you...It's...very serious...

He fell silent. The words were sticking in his throat. A flush of shame was running over his skin. M Thuillier nodded and attempted to relight his cigarette end by the flame of a flat, round lighter:

'You have problems?

'Yes, said Etienne.

'What problems?

Etienne hesitated a few seconds, half closed his eyelids, and replied in a breathy voice:

'Just now I wanted to commit suicide.

'You have my compliments, said M Thuillier.

He had succeeded in relighting his cigarette end and seemed happy with this performance.

'My dear boy, he continued, the desire to kill oneself is the privilege of superior beings. To think about suicide is to bring judgement to bear on the essentials of life. It is to undertake applied metaphysics. Animals, savages, simple minded people do not commit suicide. By contrast, every enlightened man has wondered, at least three times in his life, whether death was not preferable to the destiny he had chosen.

Etienne, who had counted on his teacher being astonished, was disappointed by this moderate speech. M Thuillier wrinkled his nostrils and continued in a playful way:

'Even so, be assured that I am happy to see you alive. Thinking about suicide is salutary. Putting the plan into action brings about awkward consequences. Revolver, poison, hanging?

'Revolver, said Etienne.

'That's easy and manly. And at the last moment, you were afraid?

Etienne looked down:

'Yes. I couldn't do it. It was stronger than me.

'Don't apologise. But why, if it is not an indiscreet question, did you want to kill yourself. A disappointment in your love life, no doubt?

'No, sir! cried Etienne.

His teacher's assumption seemed insulting. His lips were trembling. He looked straight ahead, his eyes shining with fury.

'I did not want to upset you, M Thuillier continued. It's normal that at your age...

'I told you no...

'Well, let's say no more about it. Besides, it is very difficult to determine the reason for suicide. One treads the same path for years, limited by the same horizons. One is neither happy, nor unhappy. One follows the same pattern of life: working, eating, taking the underground, going to the cinema, sleeping, counting one's money. And, suddenly, the chain of everyday actions is broken. The mind is thrown into the void. The structure wobbles. Seized with panic, the man asks himself terrible questions:

"Why? What's the point? What must I do?" It is not unusual, with young people, for the study of philosophy to trigger the crisis.

'It's not the study of philosophy which has disturbed my mind, said Etienne.

'What, then?

Etienne leaned his forearms on the armrests of the chair. He was at the top of a tower. He was going to jump. He murmured:

'I learned...I learned, a few days ago, that my father was a murderer.

M. Thuillier stubbed out his cigarette end against his heel, pulled up a chair and sat behind the table. His wide hands, with their short fingers, were crossed under his chin. His lips moved against each other.

'How interesting that is! he said.

Etienne had the impression that M Thuillier did not believe him.

'I swear it's true, sir, he said.

Looking up, M Thuillier took a ruler and scratched the nape of his neck with little strokes, as if he were handling the bow of a violin.

'And when might this event have occurred? he asked at last.

'Five years ago. At Cauterets. You didn't read in the newspapers about the trial of Louis Martin?

'Perhaps. I don't know...

'Louis Martin, said Etienne, was my father. He was judged. He was guillotined. My mother hadn't told me...

Driven by the need to arouse the person he was talking to, he related everything: the letter, the parcel, Marion's revelations, the reading of the newspapers, the trial. He surprised himself by the pleasure he was taking in confiding these matters. The interest M Thuillier was showing appeased his scruples and made the admissions easier. Forgetting all restraint, he unburdened himself, he relieved himself, of words which had been long trapped within him. He was exuding his poison through every pore of his skin.

'I hesitated for a long time to come and see you, he said. I didn't dare. I was ashamed. It's terrible living with a secret like that in your heart. Impossible to speak about it to my mother without hurting her. And none of my friends would have been capable of understanding me. You have been very kind to me. Always. I trust you. You will help me, you will advise me...There must surely be something I can do...

'What do you want to do?

'I don't know. See the lawyer. Try to determine to what extent my father was responsible. One thing is certain: he didn't kill in order to steal, contrary to what they said. But he was perhaps employed by the militia, by the Gestapo. He was acting on behalf of a political party...

'You would prefer that explanation?

'A conviction, an ideal, that excuses the worst excesses...Do you not think so?..I don't understand it at all...It's up to you to tell me...I would like to restore his good name...I would like to prove to people that they were wrong to guillotine him.

'What would that change, seeing that he's dead?

'That would change everything. I could think of him without revulsion, without worry.

'So it's in your own interest that you want to rehabilitate your father?

'My interest and his are one and the same. They reviled him. They dragged him through the mud. They cut off his head. I cannot tolerate this idea of a headless man. Sometimes I hate him and sometimes I pity him. Previously I was a bloke like the rest. And suddenly I am the son of a murderer. I had nothing to do with that. I am innocent. And it is as if I were guilty. As guilty as him. People make me fearful or they disgust me, because they do not know, because if they knew, they would avoid me. I walk around in the world like a man with the plague. I want to spit on everything, to destroy everything.

The words were coming into his mouth like big nauseous hiccoughs. His destiny, crushing him as it was, was merging with the heat, his tiredness, the droning of his voice in the room. Through a damp veil he could vaguely perceive M Thuillier's head, heavy and round, his wide mouth, his bulging eyes behind the gold framed glasses.

'I understand your distress, said M Thuillier, but I definitely advise you not to go and see the lawyer. Whatever the motive your father had for killing, the idea of a trial to rehabilitate him is unacceptable. Louis Martin still struck down two or three people. Whether to steal, or to take revenge, or to prevent their crossing the border, it doesn't change anything with respect to the law.

'So, said Etienne, I must accept their sentence, I must admit that they were right, I must thank them for having administered justice...

'I'm not asking as much as that! cried M Thuillier, raising both hands so that they were level with his ears. Protest inwardly as much as you like. But understand that this protest will only have a value in itself.

Etienne shrugged his shoulders:

'This lawyer knew my father. He saw him in prison. He spoke to him. He will be able to tell me...

'What?

'What kind of man my father was, whether I must hate him or defend him...

'I don't suppose you need the advice of a lawyer to know what you have to do.

'Yes, certainly. I can't see the situation clearly. I am going bonkers.

M Thuillier got up, walked over to Etienne, placed a hand on his shoulder.

'Listen to me carefully, Martin, he said. If I were in your place, I would be happy with what's happening to me.[1]

'Happy? Etienne stammered. Happy to be the son of a murderer?

'Why not? Forget that it concerns you. Try to reason objectively. By launching oneself into the universe, by suffering, by struggling, a man defines himself, creates himself gradually, in opposition to other men. Those we consider to be similar to us are useful, first and foremost, in demonstrating that we do not resemble them. Consequently, the fact is that we are ourselves in so far as we are not them; it is because we come up against the world that the world exists and that we exist.

'Yes, said Etienne, you have already explained that in class. But what connection does that conception of the world have with my father?

'Wait, Martin; if a man is nothing intrinsically, but creates himself by his actions, and if, in so doing, he creates the world which surrounds him and invents his own way of making use of it, how could he not be seized with fear before such a huge responsibility?

The words fell on Etienne, thick and fast. He found himself back in school, on a bench, facing the blackboard. "*Being* and *the appearance of being* ...the *prereflexive cogito*, the *transphenomenal existence...*" The memory of this time which had been happy and which he could not recover, struck a blow in his heart. M Thuillier raised a finger:

'Man struggles in the midst of chaos. He feels that it will be impossible, however intelligent he might be, to discover the precise justification of his presence on earth. Accepting this ignorance, he experiences anguish in the face of the absurdity of his condition, that no-one would be able to explain in human terms. Do you follow me?

'Certainly, sir...

"What's he driving at? I know his theory, but it's a mind game which doesn't concern me. I am in real life, profoundly, horribly. And he juggles with ideas, strings together rational arguments, struggles against shadows." Once again, he thought about the revolver. A shudder shot up from his back to his neck.

'What meaning does a man's sojourn have in the hell of pretence and contradictions? If I am persuaded that life is stupid, incoherent, limited in duration, I have to admit that the only way to live is to live at top speed. Not to be delicate, but greedy. To take double helpings. To take advantage of every opportunity that is offered to me to affirm my true nature!

He moved away from Etienne in order to see him more clearly and crossed his arms on his chest:

'Integrity, for the man who has understood the absurdity of the world, does not consist in being what others want him to be, but in what he wants to be himself. It is in being himself, as intensely as possible, that he will best use the period of time which separates his birth from his death. Whatever his destiny might be, if this destiny is freely chosen by him, it is worthy of esteem.

Etienne gestured in irritation:

'In other words, man is an end in himself. And since my father felt the need to kill, he was right to do so.

'From the point of view of the judges, of the victims, in short, of society itself, no. From his personal point of view: yes. As each person is master of his morality, your father, with respect to his conscience, is responsible, but not guilty.

'But look, sir, that's not possible, murmured Etienne.

In a flash, he had the impression that M Thuillier was making fun of him. He looked up. The teacher's face was serious, inspired. His eyes, behind his thick glasses, defied all opposition, in the present time and in the future, to his philosophy.

'And why not? he said in a harsh voice. If God does not exist, there is no *a priori* morality, all human activities are equal, one to another. Now, if all human activities are equal, we must not judge them according to the objective being pursued, but according to the determination which each individual brings to the pursuit. What is at stake counts for less than the conviction expended in achieving it. The perfect drunkard is more respectable than the imperfect priest. And being an excellent postal worker or an excellent murderer amounts to the same thing.

He raised his chin and, giving Etienne a mischievous and slippery look, with eyes the colour of liquorice, said:

'You do not agree with me? You would have preferred your father to be a failed civil servant, a lazy cobbler?...

'Yes, said Etienne, anything, but not that...

'You put me in mind of the people who, in days gone by, leaving the theatre, would be booing the actor who had the part of the traitor in the play. These dear idiots blamed the actor for the talent he had shown in the role. In a way, they resented the admiration they had for him. They hated him because he had been what he had to be. Your father was what he had to be. He committed himself to a path: *good* or *bad*, these words have no meaning. But he followed his path to the end, and that alone is what counts.

M Thuillier continued for a long time on that theme. Etienne, dazed, felt himself overcome with a sickening torpor. His limbs relaxed, hung like tresses of soft wool. His mind wandered far away, on an expanse of blue smoke. He believed for a moment that he was sleeping, that this room, these papers, this man, were coming to him in a dream.

'Now, have you understood? asked M Thuillier.

Etienne started, came back to earth.

'Yes, he said, I think so...I'm trying...But deep down, what will become of me?

'You were drifting, you were seeking your real self. You have found your true course in life.

'What course in life? I no longer know who I am.

'You are the son of a murderer. Instead of shying away from this truth, you must embrace it with gratitude.

'Which means?

'Which means that, from now on, it is important that you act no longer as the son of any old person, but as the son of "the killer of Cauterets". Do not try to forget, or to excuse or to denigrate your father. Accept him for what he is. Be proud of his crimes and of his severed head.

Etienne shook his head. It seemed to him that fish scales were flying around him:

'I shall not be able to...

'But you will, you will, it's a matter of common sense. A man must know that everything is allowed. The rewards and punishments for his actions are within himself. Remember the splendid cry of Nietzsche[2]: "I gave nobility to all things, when I said that behind them there was always an act of will." Think of all those philosophers of existential despair. Your father was clear headed about being a murderer and so he was reconciled with his conscience. You must be clear headed about being the son of a murderer; then you will find peace of mind and the joys of life.

'Joys of life?...whispered Etienne.

He thought of Marion, of Maxime Joubert. His heart tightened.

'Do you want me to read you a passage from my book? said M Thuillier.

'Yes, said Etienne.

This suggestion flattered him. M Thuillier, moving past Etienne, tapped him lightly on the back of the neck.

'If you hadn't told me what you did tell me, I would not have had the idea of reading what I'm going to read.

'Why?

'Because I would have been afraid of addressing a person slumbering in his daily customs, buried in the amorphous glue of everyday life. You were somebody else when I knew you. An ordinary, well behaved kid. A little cleverer than his mates. Prize for overall excellence, prize for philosophy, prize for this, prize for that. What does that mean? Nothing. The shock that you have suffered has brought your nerves and mind alive. Skinned, peeled, you are at last capable of understanding...

Etienne smiled weakly:

You are interested in me because I am unhappy...

'Do you know a single happy human being who is worth spending time with? asked M Thuillier.

Etienne trembled with pleasure. For his teacher he was the object of real concern, and this seemed to him to be a sign of victory. A remarkable man was giving him consideration and consequently he was entering the brotherhood of masters of philosophy. He was accessing the privilege of an exceptional sort of suffering. M Thuillier brandished in both hands a packet of handwritten sheets and began reading:

The only certainty of any worth is that of death. It is towards a promise of nothingness that each of us is travelling. But as soon as he becomes conscious of the danger represented by this stubborn march towards meeting the void, man rises up and rebels. In a universe suddenly stripped of illusions he feels an outsider. This divorce between man and human life, between the actor and the plot, gives rise to the concept of the absurd...

M Thuillier was declaiming his text with aggressive authority. The words clattered out juicily from his tongue. From time to time he looked up and Etienne felt enveloped by his attentive eyes:

'I'm not reading too quickly?

'No, no, carry on. It's exciting.

When he said that, Etienne was sincere. It seemed to him that these pages had been written just for him. In them his personal confusion was defined, explained, exalted with intelligence.

"Belief in the absurdity of existence will henceforth order our behaviour. We shall not cheat in the face of nothingness by trying to give it the face of the Eternal Father, surrounded by papier-mâché angels. We shall accept it as it is, as the negation of everything that is us. The notion of this absence will reinforce within us the concept of our presence. If we are to be something, we must be something on earth: senior civil servant or beggar, teacher of philosophy or murderer. All experiences are of equal value...

'Did you really write that? asked Etienne in a choking voice.

'Certainly, said M Thuillier.

He gave a slight smile and continued his reading.

When he had finished, Etienne looked at him in silence, with gratitude mixed with respect.

'Well? asked M Thuillier, what do you think?

'Wonderful. cried Etienne. It is exactly what I feel. I would swear that this chapter has been inspired by our conversation.

'I am very happy to confirm that we are in agreement, said M Thuillier. Would you like a cigarette?

Etienne took a cigarette from the cigarette case which M Thuillier held over the table. A flame leaped from the lighter.

'Go on, Martin.

"He's offering me a light, thought Etienne. We are two friends, two brothers. A light feeling of intoxication overcame him. He drew on his cigarette. A wisp of smoke passed in front of his eyes. M Thuillier looked at his watch.

'It must be very late, said Etienne. And I'm holding you up, preventing you eating...

'I don't have dinner at a particular time, said M Thuillier. In the evening I eat something in a small bar near here. If you would like to join me...

'Unfortunately my mother is expecting me, said Etienne.

'Well, that's a pity. Another time...

Frustrated, Etienne stared at the toes of his shoes. At last he murmured:

'I could perhaps telephone her, tell her I'm eating with you...

'Certainly, said M Thuillier, that's an excellent idea.

Side by side, they went down the staircase of the block of flats, the steps of which were covered by linoleum imitating the irregular veins of marble. Etienne stopped at the caretaker's room to telephone his mother. She had just returned home.

'At last, my darling, she cried. I was worried. I was wondering where you had got to.

He experienced a shock deep down, hearing this familiar, lilting voice. In the company of M Thuillier, he had gone as far as forgetting the part of his existence which was devoted to Marion. Was it possible that she had carried on living, somewhere in Paris, carefree, unknowing, while he was thinking about suicide and confessing everything, without any shame, to his teacher?

'Hello, Etienne!...What?...You've changed your mind?...You've gone out?...Have you eaten at least?...

This futile question amused him: "This is a perfect example of absurdity rising up in the business of everyday life."

'No, mum, he said. But I'm going to eat. With M Thuillier. I met him by chance. Don't wait for me...

'Fine, my darling...That's M Thuillier, your philosophy teacher?..Don't be too late back...I shan't sleep until I know you're home...I love you... very, very much...

He hung up, eager to turn his back on a person he refused to be and whose memory his mother, by her remarks, wished to perpetuate.

They went into a sort of fast food café, with a low ceiling and yellow mirrors. Ten or so customers were sitting on stools at the counter. Others were eating in the room, close together, elbow to elbow, at small round tables with raffia place mats. A fan, with wide, dark blades, like the wings of a bird of prey, was slowly turning as it watched over its flock. You could hear the hissing of the percolator and the tinkling of spoons, thrown haphazardly into a metal basin. Etienne and M Thuillier sat down at the counter, on seats shaped like mushrooms.

'It's cheaper here than in the room, said M Thuillier. And the food is just as good.

In front of them, on the beige coloured wall, were stuck photographs of actors, writers and politicians. But above each portrait was a picture depicting an animal – goat, dog, horse, camel, giraffe – which had some resemblance to the character to which it was attached. This decorative idea seemed to Etienne to be charmingly novel and insolent. M Thuillier snapped his fingers and the waiter hurried up. His face was pink and there was sweat in the folds of his smile:

'Hello, M Thuillier. Do you want to see the menu?

'Wait! said M Thuillier, pointing his forefinger towards the plate of a customer sitting at the other end of the counter. What's that yellow stuff over there?

'Ratatouille niçoise, said the waiter.

'Do you fancy that? asked M Thuillier, turning towards Etienne.

'Oh! Yes, sir, said Etienne. That will be very good.

He was amazed to see M Thuillier move with such ease from the realm of philosophy to that of food.

'Right, said M Thuillier, the ratatouille it is. And with that I shall have a brandy with water. What are you drinking, Martin?

'The same, sir.

The waiter brought two glasses of brandy, two plates of ratatouille and a siphon. They started eating. M Thuillier would stab large stringy mouthfuls with his fork and chew them voraciously. You could see the bones of his jaw moving.

'It's really a very pleasant place, said Etienne. Do you often come here?

'Every evening, said M Thuillier, wiping his mouth with a paper serviette. Besides, most of the customers are regulars. I know them as if I had modelled them myself in dough.

'That must be entertaining.

'It's terrible, said M Thullier. He squirted seltzer water into the two glasses.

'Terrible? asked Etienne. Why?

'Because, brought together purely by chance in this place, they represent a perfect selection of mediocre failure, secret ugliness and heartbreaking uselessness. The tall bloke with the shining skull sitting near the door is in the final stages of syphilis. His neighbour, the fat old bag, is just out of prison. Corrupting minors or drug trafficking, I can't remember which. The young man shaking his gin and lemon works as a docker to pay for his studies. The gentleman with the curly moustache lives with a woman who is paralysed. He takes her out in his little car from two o'clock in the afternoon until seven in the evening. That elegant woman with peroxide blond hair has a drunkard of a husband who beats her black and blue. Here a dishonoured cheque, there a stomach ulcer. There, again, someone with holes in his pockets and another who is impotent. Ah! Humanity is not beautiful. It is not happy. It is not good. And yet a whole bunch of priests, of poets, of inspired odd bods would have us believe in the existence of a benevolent God. They talk of the virtues of the soul, of peace, of hope, of preordained harmony. What a load of old rubbish!

He emptied his glass in a single swallow and clicked his tongue.

'When you compare your anguish with that of others, you must feel in a state of superiority. They have the miseries of servants. You have an inner turmoil worthy of a king. Don't drag your torment around like a lead ball tied to your feet. Carry it in your arms, hold it tight against your heart, like a precious object. Let it be on your bedside table when you go to sleep, next to your plate when you are eating, near your right hand when you want to write. Each of us suffers in some way. Your suffering is enviable, Martin.

'And you, sir, asked Etienne, what do you suffer from?

'I suffer from insomnia, said M Thuillier.

Etienne averted his eyes. M Thuillier pushed his plate away. His lips, fleshy and pink, separated in a contemptuous smile:

'What would you like now? A noodle dish, an omelette, or just a dessert? I've eaten enough.

'Me too, said Etienne.

'Well then, we shall choose a dessert. Lemon ice cream? Yes? Two lemon ice creams, waiter...

A young woman, heavily made up, came lolloping across the room.

'She told her friend that she was going to make a telephone call, whispered M Thuillier. Now, she's going to the toilet. That's obvious. Look how she's squeezing her thighs together. Nothing amuses me more than to expose the hypocrisy of our fellow human beings. Call things by their name. Never forget that the most beautiful girl in the world carries eight metres of intestines in her adorable little belly.

He sighed:

'No concessions, Martin. Live with your eyes wide open, it's the secret of the great destinies.

The young woman disappeared behind the door of frosted glass. Etienne experienced an unpleasant feeling of revulsion and sadness. It seemed to him that a veil had fallen, which, previously, was separating him from the world. Now he saw things and people in the harsh light of truth. "Poor race. They do not even know who Kant is. They have never heard of Kirkegaard[2] and Jaspers[3]. They are unaware of the absurdity exemplified by the limited and incoherent period of time they spend on this patch of land. They are asleep, but I am awake. Me, with *my inner turmoil worthy of a king*." He stuck his spoon in the lemon ice cream which the waiter had just placed in front of him. A sour flavour melted on his tongue. It was nice. "My father is a murderer. I nearly killed myself. And I'm eating a lemon ice cream. Really, life is absurd." The noise of water flushing made him jump. The glass door opened again. The young woman came back into the room, an innocent smile on her lips. M Thuillier winked:

'What did I tell you?

"He's right, thought Etienne. As always. What a man!"

'Alright? asked M Thuillier.

'Certainly, said Etienne.

A cold sweat ran down his temples. M Thuillier paid the bill. Etienne wanted to pay his share.

"No, no, said M Thuillier, this evening you are my guest.

They went out together. A damp, blue night enveloped them. In the trees along the Boulevard St Germain the light from the lampposts ruffled the swathes of bright green foliage. Here and there large neon signs lit up the fronts of the sleeping houses. Passers-by flowed in groups along the pavement.

'You are not thinking any more about suicide? asked M Thuillier.

'No, said Etienne.

M Thuillier burst out laughing:

'I was sure you weren't! You are above that. You must attack life at full pelt.

Etienne thought about the ratatouille, about the girl coming out of the toilets, about the photographs of animals stuck to the beige coloured walls. A swirl of rubbish surrounded him, cradled him, as if he had swum in the dirty water of a seaport. Suddenly he felt in a hurry to be back in his bedroom.

'It's time for me to go, he said. I promised my mother that I wouldn't be back too late.

M Thuillier shook his hand vigorously:

'Come and see me again...

Etienne thanked his teacher and walked off quickly into the night.

Chapter Nine

The following morning, having swallowed a cup of milky coffee and given her instructions to the two dressmakers, Marion went back to bed. She was tired and wanted to rest a little. Etienne visited her in her room:

'You don't need anything, mum?

'Not at all. Anyway, I'm feeling better. I'm working...

Fashion magazines were strewn around her on the almond green satin bedspread.

On her knees, drawn up to act as a desk, a notebook of sketches was open. She held a pencil in her hand.

'I have been inspired by the collection which I saw last Thursday with Daisy. It's nice, isn't it?

He turned the pages. Beneath his indifferent eyes, a regiment of thin women, wearing narrow dresses, was on parade.

'That's an adorable little coat in a loose-fitting form, as you can see, in a mustard coloured, hound's tooth woollen material. The dress next to it is in grey jersey wool, pleated at the front. On the shoulders, a chestnut brown suede cape, with a woollen lining picking up the shade of the dress...

While she was speaking, he turned his head and cast his eyes briefly over the modern bedside table, in sycamore, with a mirror at the top. The revolver was there, hidden in a drawer. Etienne smiled. The memory of contact with the cold, round object made his right cheek go numb.

Here's an evening outfit. I think it's extraordinary. You can't visualise it like that. Imagine a figure hugging dress in peacock blue velvet, with green highlights, which flares out towards the base. The fullness begins from the hips.

He leaned over his mother and kissed her forehead. as one might caress, absent-mindedly, a child surrounded by toys.

'It's very pretty, Marion.

'Which do you prefer?

'I don't know.

'You surprise me: you always have such distinct ideas on fashion!...

'Alright, this one, he said, placing his finger on a sketch at random.

'The same as me, she cried. I shall transform the design in my own style and I'm sure that Mme Ortoli will be delighted. She asked me for a little practical costume for morning wear...

She yawned, showing her small, pink mouth, and stretched out her arms before her. A bed jacket, in knitted white wool, covered her shoulders. She had no make up on.

'I'm going, said Etienne.

'Where to?

'To my bedroom.

'To do what?

'Read, write a little.

'You don't want to stay with me?

'Of course, mum...

He sat down on a large pouffe, looked down and rested his elbows on his knees. Marion frowned:

'Listen, Etienne, I find you strange with me. I am your mother but also your friend. You must be able to speak frankly with me.

What was she driving at? He feared that she was going to start a difficult conversation again.

'I'm not hiding anything from you, he murmured.

'What did you do yesterday evening?

'I've already told you...

'Yes, yes... But you won't convince me that it's not odd that a teacher should invite a former pupil to a restaurant!

'Why should it be odd?

'Because...because it's not usually done...

He began laughing, relieved of a great worry:

'You don't know M Thuillier. He's different from the rest. A character. Completely out of the ordinary.

'And you were alone?...Just the two of you.

'Of course!

'I wonder what you could have been talking about.

'Philosophy!

'Oh! This philosophy! she said..

She raised her eyes to the ceiling.

'You don't like philosophy? asked Etienne.

'Why should I like it? It doesn't seem to me to be of any use. If doctors or engineers, for example, had made no progress for centuries, the world wouldn't be what it is today. But if philosophers had never existed, I would still carry on living as I do.

'That's where you're wrong, he said with passion. Philosophy is as useful to humanity as science. Without philosophy we would live like dogs. If you think about the next day, you are already engaged in philosophy. Science proves our worthlessness!

'Don't get carried away, my darling.

'Just think, Marion, he continued, suddenly standing up. The teaching of astronomy, biology can only inspire us with complete, miserable, sterile humility in the face of the dimension of outer space, or in the face of the laws of the preservation of species. Caught between the infinitely great and the infinitely small, aware of the brief duration of his existence and the futility of his works, man ought to decide, with clear-sightedness, that all effort is useless, and that it's better just to sit around doing nothing. If he overcomes this state of unhealthy prostration, it's because philosophy allows him to find, in the very depths of his despair, pride in understanding and accepting...

'What gibberish! cried Marion. You are reciting a lesson.

He blushed. Indeed, his words were not his own, but served as an introduction to M Thuillier's lesson on metaphysics.

'Whether they are my words, or someone else's, is not important. They express my profound conviction. Have you never wondered if life has a meaning and what you have to do to use, to the maximum, the possibilities you have of affirming that meaning?

A ring at the bell resounded in the hall. Etienne felt a pang of impatience, but he steadied himself and went on, raising his voice:

'We are the sum of the actions we choose. You create yourself and I create myself, starting from a blank page. Nietzsche said: "It is clearly apparent that the principal thing in heaven and on earth is to obey, in the long term and in the same direction..." To change direction is to be lost. All paths in life are one way. you don't go back...

A second ring at the bell interrupted him.

'Mme Marthe hasn't heard, said Marion. You should go and see...

He came back to earth from afar.

'Quickly, my love, Marion repeated.

Etienne suppressed within himself a seething mass of deeply felt words, gave an angry look and went rapidly out of the room. In the hall the humming of the sewing machine filled his ears. He opened the front door and stood there, amazed. In front of him was a boy of about fifteen years of age, who gripped in his arms a spray of red roses, wrapped in transparent paper.

'Mme Loiselet, asked the boy, is this the right flat?

'Yes, said Etienne.

The boy handed him the bouquet. Etienne rummaged in his pocket and dropped a few coins in the delivery boy's hand.

'Thank you, sir, said the lad.

The door closed with a thud. Etienne trembled. A strange unease pressed on his stomach. Marion's voice called out

'What is it, Etienne?

He crossed the hall and went back into the bedroom, ceremoniously carrying before him the gift from another man. Sitting in her bed, Marion was watching the arrival of this ensemble of vivid petals, crumpled foliage and fine paper. An expression of childlike gratitude smoothed the skin of her cheek and gave a radiance to her eyes. Etienne put the bouquet down on the bedspread.

'They are wonderful! said Marion.

Already, with expert hands, she was removing the pins, unfolding the wrapping, revealing to the light a brash profusion of green and crimson colours. A sweet perfume, vaguely soap like, filled the room.

'Wonderful, wonderful! Marion repeated. What extravagance!

With a flick of her finger nail, she opened the small white envelope which accompanied the bouquet. A visiting card fell on her knees. She took it between her thumb and forefinger, raised it to her eyes, tossed it on her bedside table, and a mysterious smile changed her features. Etienne felt, with a painful precision, that a stranger had just entered her mind and that everything was lighting up to receive him. As far as he, Etienne, was concerned, dethroned, banished, he could not bring himself to give way. He remained there, with his useless philosophical arguments, his gravity no longer appropriate, his austerity now out of place.

'I shall put them in the big blue vase, she murmured.

'Yes, said Etienne, that will be very nice.

Marion pushed back the blankets and slipped out of bed. You could sense her slight yet chubby body under her flowing nightdress. She had red nail varnish on her toes.

'Do you want me to fetch the vase? asked Etienne

'No, no, wait here.

She went out and closed the door. After a moment he could hear a sound of voices and he realised that Marion was speaking on the 'phone. She had not been able to wait a minute longer to thank the one who had given the gift. Etienne took the visiting card from the bedside table and read: *Maxime Joubert*. Beneath this name, in large characters, were a few words rapidly written in purple ink: *See you this evening Marion*. A sudden contraction gripped Etienne's jaw. In this bedroom, previously under his power, the red roses, the transparent paper, the visiting card were joining forces against him and destroying his chances of success.

How could Marion allow herself to be taken in by a such a common sort of compliment? She had been the wife of Louis Martin. She was still marked in her flesh, in her soul, by the revelation of the crimes he had committed. And today she was preparing to trade this sombre dignity for the advantages of a few francs. "She's mad. She does not understand the new beginning she has been given. She is negligent of, unaware of, the delights of solitude, of horror. She wants to start a new life. You do not start a new life. You create it. If my destiny consists of being, with increasing consciousness, the son of a murderer, Marion's destiny is to be fulfilled, in all its actions, as the wife of the same person. Everything else is only show, a waste of time, and a mistake in the way she conducts herself." He replaced the visiting card on the bedside table. Behind the door a murmur continued, annoying and embarrassing. Etienne put his ear to the door: "You've spoilt me...You shouldn't have...I'm going to put them in a lovely blue vase..."

He went over to the window and breathed the air in deeply to combat the unease which was oppressing him. "Has she even told him that she is the divorced wife of a murderer? Surely not. She's ashamed of it. But she isn't ashamed of these flowers, of these dinner invitations, of this futile, idiotic, degrading life." In the hall, Marion had stopped speaking. He turned round. His glance took in the unmade bed, the roses, a corner of the bedroom given over to happiness. He wished that an explosion would reduce this pleasant scene to fragments. "Is it still possible to extract her from this grip of pleasure, to bring her back, trembling, repentant, to Louis Martin's furrow?" She returned. Transfigured. You would have thought that she had put on make up in the time she had been out of the room. She held in both hands, like a censer, the blue vase full of water. Without saying a word, she placed it on the bedside table, and, taking the roses one by one, she placed them carefully in the receptacle. Then she took a step back to judge the effect.

'They have a very distinctive colour, very warm, she said at last.

Etienne felt that it was not the right moment to resume the conversation. Sluggishly he moved towards the door.

'Are you going? she asked, getting back into bed.

Too overcome with emotion to reply, he nodded.

She assumed a guilty expression and said hurriedly:

'You won't be pleased with me, Etienne, but I have to go out this evening. You will be on your own for dinner.

'No, he said.

'Why?

'I'm also going out.

'With friends?

He thought for a few seconds and replied abruptly:

'With M Thuillier.

'Again!

'Yes, he promised to read me some more chapters from his book.

'And you enjoy that?

'As much as you enjoy having dinner in town.

She did not react to the rudeness. She had assumed a dreamy expression.

A brief thoughtful pout creased her lips. Next to her, the red, velvety bouquet absorbed all the sunlight. Etienne was tired and sad, keen to be alone, yet full of apprehension in the face of the long day which stretched before him. He left the room without Marion making the slightest gesture for him to stay.

*

For the third time, Etienne rang the bell. There was only a hollow silence. M Thuillier had gone out. "Yet he told me that I would find him at home every day in the late afternoon. So, what is the time?" Before leaving home Etienne had put on Louis Martin's wrist watch. He looked at it: seven o'clock. The leather strap, narrow and worn, compressed his veins a little under his skin. The catch was in a hole widened by use. "I have the same size wrist as my father, thought Etienne. It's funny." He had also brought the photograph to show to M Thuillier. "Wait here for him to come back? Have a look in the restaurant where we had dinner? I must see him. Without fail." His need to meet M Thuillier was becoming insistent, like a physical requirement. No-one but that man was capable of understanding him, of helping him. Slowly he descended the staircase, sliding his hand along the polished wood bannister rail. The marbling of the linoleum danced before his eyes, like patches of foam on the sea. "And at the present time there are people bathing, sprawled on the sand, in the sun. They call that: holidays..."

A hundred metres from the house, on the same side of the street, the doors of the fast food cafe, both open, exuded a smell of cooking. Bravely, Etienne entered and made his way between the tables. Suddenly his courage failed him. Opposite him he saw M Thuillier, sitting with two men and a woman, in front of a small, round table covered with glasses. The teacher's complexion was bright red, his glasses were shining. He was speaking with exceptional fluency. Those listening to him were people of his age. One of the gentlemen even had grey hair, the other was half bald. As for the woman, her graceless face was brightened by a thick layer of make up. Suddenly she burst out laughing. The unknown bald man leaned back in his chair.

M Thuillier smiled triumphantly, drank a mouthful of cloudy liquid from the glass he held in his hand, and carried on speaking in a low voice. Philosophy, politics, literature? From where he stood, Etienne could not properly hear the remarks being exchanged a few paces from him. But he could read on his teacher's face the signs of obvious intellectual excitement. In all probability, M Thuillier was using, in order to captivate these strangers, the same virtues of fervour, of eloquence which he had employed, the day before, in convincing his former pupil. As if stripped of a mysterious privilege, Etienne was watching this talkative person drifting away from him, gradually entering the everyday, mundane world. Odd phrases floated to the surface of the general conversation:

'You should write a mean little article which will rile him...Oswald doesn't deserve anything else. I don't give a damn about Christian Existentialism....If the *Editions de Boeuf* want to fund the journal...

Etienne thought that M Thuillier's friends were perhaps important people: journalists, publishers. In their company M Thuillier would no doubt have forgotten the young man who had come and pestered him yesterday evening with stories of near suicide. "I no longer matter to him. He's thinking of something else. He's drinking, eating, chatting. He's among people who are forty, forty-five. Whatever I might do, I shall only be a kid in his eyes. It's with others, with old people, that he feels at ease. You've only got to look at him..." The waiter, passing by, bumped into Etienne:

'There's room at the bar, sir.

'Thank you, said Etienne, I'm looking for someone.

His face was burning. He remained standing, between two tables, like a wooden post. Incapable of moving. Rebellious, unhappy. "I'll leave.

No, I'll stay. He will see me. He will call me...What's the point, now?

The waiter returned, balancing a tray above his head. Etienne moved back to let him pass. And, suddenly, M Thuillier, looking up, noticed him. It was like a ray of sunshine. Etienne smiled. M Thuillier waved aloft his soft, grey hand:

'Hello, Martin.

'Good evening, sir, said Etienne.

Already, M Thuillier had looked away. The woman with the made up face was speaking in his ear. His face took on a scandalised expression and he roared with laughter.:

'No? You're joking! Oswald said that?

The noise of the room became deafening. Etienne made his way towards the door. He was whistling to give an impression of composure. The street was noisy and misty, dominated by an early dusk, the colour of violets. Etienne walked on the kerb. One car followed another. Silhouettes of people flowed incessantly along. All "oldies". It was old people who made the world. The success of old people was unacceptable. Their logic made you shudder. If Louis Martin had murdered three collaborators, he would today have been considered a hero of the Liberation. By the same token, if the Germans had won the war and if Louis Martin's victims had been leaders of the Resistance, he would have been decorated in the *Cour des*

Invalides for services to the Fatherland. But Louis Martin had received no command from anyone, spoken in English, French, German, to sacrifice a defenceless man. And suddenly there was no excuse for his criminal obstinacy. The allied partisans and the German partisans came together to spit on his corpse. When he thought about the time of the occupation and the purge, Etienne could see, in his mind's eye, a confusion of names, one minute held in adulation and the next in shame. Someone who was a person of high rank one day was judged to be a perfect bastard the next. The most well established positions would collapse into a morass of muck and blood. Prisons changed their inmates, newspapers their headlines, flags their colour; and money changed hands.

At that time, at school, in the street, Etienne's friends, twelve years old like him, would play Nazi militiamen and patriots. Rulers or pencil boxes, fixed in the bend of the arm, would represent submachine guns firing their bullets. Paratroopers in short trousers refused to give up their secrets to dunces playing the part of torturers, armed with a pair of compasses and a plumb line. A tribunal of school kids, meeting behind a newspaper kiosk, would condemn a traitor whose pockets were stuffed full of marbles. They shot people, denounced people, worked for the Resistance, or fought, as a joke. And yet, in the previous generation, "grown ups" lived in all seriousness in the same incoherence of actions and feelings. They played, like their sons, like their daughters, but their decisions resulted in a real bullet in real flesh.

Etienne detested "the grown ups". He reproached them for their vanity, their gratuitous stupidity, their bogus experience and their cruelty. It was "the grown ups" who had invented Work and Rewards, Money and Marriage, the *Légion d'honneur* and the Guillotine. "Is it possible that one day I might become like them, imbued with prejudices and impervious to criticism? Is it possible that M Thuillier should be on the side of the "grown ups"? If that is so, I shall never see him again as long as I live. Anyway, he's not keen to meet up with me. I understood that well enough just now. He gave me some advice for every occasion. And now he is no longer interested in me. 'Sort yourself out with what I've told you. Look for the solution within yourself.' I am alone, alone..."
He repeated this word, walking to the dull rhythm of a big drum.

'Alone, alone, alone...

"Nobody at home. Nobody in town. What shall I do? Where shall I eat? How shall I kill the time until the magical hour of sleep? Thrusting forward his chin, Etienne and his thoughts marched forward, as if on parade, in front of the Saint-Germain-des-Pres Church. The huge steeple, the colour of a porous moon, watched over the humdrum bustle of the square. At the policeman's signal, the cars came to a halt, straining with impatience, in order to allow the pedestrians to cross the carriageway. Etienne followed the flow, stepped onto the pavement opposite and continued his walk. Then, suddenly, he stopped. And all his thoughts stopped behind him, in a confused hubbub, thoughts that were clashing one with another and making no progress.

'Martin, Martin!

Someone was shouting his name. His father's name. He swivelled round to face the challenge. A hand held out, a smile. It was a classmate, Maroussel, dishevelled, suntanned, strongly built, his shirt collar open on a chest covered with tattoos.

'What the hell are you doing here, Martin?

'I was having a walk.

'Come and have a drink. I'm at the *Flore* with my brother, with Palaiseau and some mates...

'Oh, really? said Etienne. I didn't know you were already back from your holiday...

Nothing had prepared him for this meeting with a representative of human mediocrity. As if he had been addressed in a language which was not his own, Etienne was looking for words before replying and trying, out of politeness, to put himself on a level with this dull witted stranger.

'Well, are you coming?, continued Maroussel.

Etienne wanted to refuse, but the thought of being at a loose end seemed excruciating. Wasn't the company of a few amusing boys preferable to the silent punishment of his loneliness? On the corner of the street, in a little glass cage, an automatic machine was making popcorn. The grains of maize, bursting forth, bombarded the glass. Etienne breathed in a sugary aroma.

'Alright, he said, but I won't stay long.

Maroussel took him by the arm and led him towards the cafe terrace. The drinkers formed a rectangle of compact flesh. It looked as if they had been packed together in a cattle truck beforehand and, when the casing had been removed, they were continuing, out of habit, to huddle tightly together in a restricted space. Etienne and his friend slipped between the small round marble tables to the noisy group, who were gesturing to them to approach. Maroussel's elder brother, a medical student, wore a thin, narrow beard on his pink cheeks, which were satin smooth. Horn-rimmed glasses and a pipe in the form of a question mark added manliness to his face. Next to him, Palaiseau was chewing on a straw with the self-satisfied expression of a cow. Biosque and Kellermann, two former philosophy pupils, were also sitting at the same table. Between them were two girls he did not know. One was blond and pale, her face sleepy looking; the other, brunette and plump, with a surly and determined appearance, was laughing stupidly and showing her tongue.

Paulette Mauricet and Yolande Strass, said Maroussel.

Etienne greeted them awkwardly. They made space for him. Maroussel drew up a chair.

'What are you having to drink? Martin, asked Palaiseau.

'A brandy with water, said Etienne.

He had never been to the *Cafe de Flore*. Amused, his eyes scanned the array of eccentric and idle humanity. In this place of intellectual encounters it seemed to him that each individual was anxious to present himself as a caricature of the person he was. As he glanced around haphazardly, he noticed, by turns, an ecstatic girl, with a hard face the colour of flint, a boy with a shaved head whose body was encased in a cowboy shirt with squares, a suburban prophet with a flowing blond beard, a black woman with thick lips, a Chinese man with a severe nervous tic. They were all drinking, all speaking in a loud voice. People were coming in and going out. The rumbling of cars and the tinkling of saucers increased the impression of chaos and absurdity exuded by this spectacle in the open air.

'You know, said Palaiseau, I'm going to flog my bike and buy a vélo-solex.[1]

'Well, said Maroussel, my brother has promised to let me have his motorbike.

'I wouldn't be so sure about that, said his elder brother, I still need it. Dad's Citroen guzzles too much petrol.

'In three weeks, the new term! groaned Kellermann. You don't give a damn about that, ladies?

He leaned towards Etienne and explained with authority:

'Yolande is a typist in a news agency. Paulette is looking for work. If you spot something for her...

'So, it's settled, Maroussel, asked Biosque, you've signed up for a Business Studies diploma?

'Yes, replied Maroussel. And what about you, what are you aiming at?

'English degree. Afterwards, we shall see.

'You're right, said Kellermann. Languages, my friend, languages, that's the only reliable thing!

Both girls burst out laughing. Kellermann blushed. The elder Maroussel choked on the smoke from his pipe.

'Well said, Kellermann. And Martin, what is he planning to do?

'Law, said Etienne.

'There are not a lot of openings there, said Biosque. Civil Service or a barrister?

'Wait a minute, his degree may help him get into a bank, declared Palaiseau, spitting into his hand the straw he had been chewing for ten minutes.

'The only profitable way of getting into a bank, replied Maroussel, is at night, a break in.

Once again, the two girls howled with laughter.

'I don't intend to begin my career in a bank, said Etienne. I want to be a barrister.

'Commercial law? asked Maroussel's brother.

'A criminal barrister, said Etienne.

Yolande, the brunette, looked at him in amazement:

'You will defend criminals?

'Yes, said Etienne.

He was hot. His heart was pounding.

'That must be exciting, continued the girl. You see dramas. You get inside twisted minds...

'I wonder, said Maroussel's brother, if it isn't depressing in the long run, for a barrister to spend his time and energy defending flawed human beings.

A wave of anger rose to Etienne's lips:

'Is it depressing for a doctor – seeing you want to be a doctor – to spend all his life studying rotten organs?

'Excuse me, my friend, you can't compare...

'Every human being deserves to be protected from death, whether this death is the result of the progress of an illness or the application of a law!

'So, in your opinion, the barrister, who, thanks to his talent, saves the life of a murderer, is as necessary for the structure of society, as the doctor who achieves the cure of an honest man?

'Absolutely. Besides, if you were called to the bedside of a murderer, would you refuse to treat him?

'No, said the elder Maroussel, scowling, I wouldn't refuse.

'So, concluded Etienne, we are agreed. Confronted with a human being who is suffering, whatever crimes he is accused of, the barrister and the doctor come together in the same duty to humanity.

He stopped talking, amazed by his own eloquence. His whole face was burning, as under the light from a projector.

There's no getting away from it, sighed Palaiseau, that bloke Martin talks like a book…

The elder Maroussel gave a half smile. Clearly, he was annoyed by not having the final word in the discussion.

'A delightful paradox, he said, but a paradox all the same.

Then, to turn the conversation in another direction, he spoke about international politics. He had precise ideas on the expansion of communism in the Far East. Biosque cried:

'We have been born into a rotten era! One thing seems clear to me. Statesmen are the enemy of youth.

'To desire the greatness of a country is to admit the necessity for wholesale massacres, agreed Kellermann. Now, no idea is worth sacrificing your life for.

The younger Maroussel was not of this view. He thought that war had a good side. One of his uncles had done great things in the Resistance:

'That bloke, let me tell you, I consider him a hero. For him, France is everything. When he speaks about honour, you feel that he is stirred to the depths of his being. One day he was nicked by two Huns in the Bois de Vincennes. He killed them both. With a cosh…

'And now, asked Etienne, what does he do?

'He makes fridges.

'And he's been decorated?

'Of course.

'Because he killed someone.

'Because he did his duty.

'Duty is a relative concept, said Etienne. It is imposed by men on other men. It changes according to circumstances and governments.

'You are preaching anarchy!

'He's right, said Biosque. Let them leave us in peace. Let them allow us to live as we wish. Isn't that right, my darling?

He leaned towards Paulette and kissed her furtively on the neck.

'These young ladies find us completely bloody annoying, said Maroussel senior. And, between ourselves, they aren't wrong. What shall we do?

'Let's have dinner in the Chinese restaurant, suggested Biosque.

'Not a great idea, said Kellermann. If we made do with a sandwich, we could finish the evening at the *Fisto*.

'Oh! yes, cried Yolande, clapping her hands.

'I'm completely skint, said Palaiseau.

"We'll sort things out. Cards on the table. Count your money.

They put their money together and Maroussel senior promised to cover most of the expense.

'If the need arises, I shall write a cheque, he announced.

Paulette looked at him, radiant and astonished.:

'You have a bank account?

'It's essential! he said, looking exasperated.

It was ten o'clock in the evening, when the whole gang, pushing each other and laughing, hurried down the steep stone staircase which led to the basement of the *Fisto*. Although he had often heard about the place, Etienne was surprised by the spectacle of this low cellar, crowded, yet sweet smelling. On a platform, the young people of the band, in shirt sleeves, were blowing, fit to burst, into gleaming metal instruments. A weak light shone from a few ceiling lamps with oil-paper shades. The walls were decorated with red and black prints of feet, hands and lips. It seemed as if a storm had torn these features from the customers and crushed them, haphazardly, against the walls. A waiter approached the group of newcomers. He smiled broadly.

'A table?

'Yes, shouted the elder Maroussel. And in a good position.

When they had settled themselves around two small circular tables, near the dance floor, the manager of the café came to take their order. Whisky for everybody, commanded the elder Maroussel. And you can give us a discount for a bulk order. It was Gaston who recommended us.

'Who's Gaston? asked Yolande, when the manager had left.

'Nobody. I said Gaston. I might as well have said Albert. But it works every time.

He clicked his tongue and relit his pipe, which was not drawing well. Etienne, stifled by a wave of heat and noise which seemed to cover him, was trying to get his breath, and blinking nervously. In front of him, in a cloud of steam, forty people were jigging about to the sound of an hysterical trumpet. Gripped by frenzy, boys, glistening with sweat, were manhandling girls, who were dishevelled, with eyes distracted and breasts hanging loosely. With a brisk thrust, a black man, uncoordinated in his movements, threw, far from him, his lightweight companion, caught her again, dispatched her, changed her into a flag, into a whirlwind, into a puff of smoke, and suddenly gave her back her human appearance of a little student tired out by the escapade. Next to him a plump cherub, his shirt out of his trousers, was leaping about in dazzling fashion in front of his partner whose eyes were the colour of liquorice. Two women were dancing together, and laughter flowed from their open mouths as water pours from bottles. Occasionally, some of the dancers, defeated by the rhythm, would stop by common assent, and form a circle around a lithe and earnest couple, who were inventing difficult steps.

'Good health! said the elder Maroussel.

Etienne brought the glass of whisky to his lips. Kellermann and Biosque stood up:

'Let's get moving, ladies...

The two girls obediently followed their partners and, with them, plunged into the pulsating mass of dancers.

'Can you dance, Martin? asked Palaiseau.

'No. Well, vaguely. And not this stuff.

'I was like you. Yolande taught me. That girl is fantastic. Fantastic energy.

"What am I doing here? thought Etienne. How can my inner drama reconcile itself with this madhouse?" He looked at his watch. Inanimate objects were comfortable everywhere. Etienne envied inert matter. He wanted to be insignificant and indifferent, something which has no feeling and is not out of place anywhere.

The seconds passed, and he could not turn his attention away from the watch. This banal strap was the only thing which linked him to his father. It was like one side of a pair of handcuffs. The other side gripped Louis Martin's wrist. The murderer and his son, chained together, seated side by side.

The elder Maroussel ordered another round of whiskies. The ground vibrated as at the edge of a turbine engine. Biosque and Kellermann, out of breath, wilting, led their partners back to the table.

'The bloke on the sax is top notch, said Biosque.

Yolande was plastering her damp face, using a powder puff.

'Yolande, said Palaiseau, you will have to take charge of Martin.

Etienne trembled:

'No...why?..

'He can't dance, continued Palaiseau.

'And he wants me to teach him? asked Yolande

There was a touch of irony in her voice. Etienne murmured:

'It's not worth the bother, Yolande, I assure you...

The girl frowned. She drew her lips together, so that her mouth resembled a small strawberry the colour of blood.

'And if I would like to teach you?..

'Ah! She's shut you up! cried Palaiseau.

'Let me have a breather first. It can get really packed in this place!

Having eaten little and drunk a great deal, Etienne had a headache. He wanted to fish out the small ice cube floating in his drink and rub his temples with it. But he did not dare. The elder Maroussel had placed his arm around Paulette's waist and was fingering the tips of her breasts. comfortably. She let him do it, her eyes closed, her expression serious, as if she were attentive to a very important phenomenon within her. The younger Maroussel, exhausted by the music and the heat, was dozing, collapsed on his chair, his mouth gaping and his ears red. Palaiseau kicked Etienne in the calf.

'Make the most of your situation, he said quietly. You're the only one in the race now. The others have had enough.

A feeling of dizziness rose from Etienne's stomach to his forehead, which broke out in an abundant sweat.

'Bugger off, he muttered.

'Blow me, you can be an idiot! said Palaiseau.

Etienne wondered with pleasure, with horror, what would happen in this room, if he were to jump on a table and, facing the dancers, facing the band, shout out that he was the son of a murderer. He imagined the jostling, then the indignant silence his admission would provoke. Impersonal mouths, deformed by fear and hatred, surrounding him. A cry rising up from all these honest breasts: "Get out! Get out!" He clenched his fists. "It's obvious. I have the right to stay here only on condition that I hide my real identity. These strangers accept my presence among them because they do not know my background. The politeness of the waiters, the indifference of the people, the concern my friends have for me, all that is based on a misunderstanding.

One word from my mouth would be enough to create a void around me. But this word I shall not pronounce. Because I am a coward. Because I need the society which condemned my father. Because I can live without my father, but I could not live without society.

He reflected again, intently, and clarified his thoughts more precisely: "Yes, that's it exactly, as long as I am ashamed of my father, honest people will not be ashamed of me. In choosing to frequent them, I choose, by the same token, to deny my father."

Never before had the idea of this necessary choice presented itself so clearly to his mind. With them, against him. Or with him, against them. No compromise possible. No zigzags. A straight line. He raised his glass, drank, without pleasure, the lukewarm and bitter liquid it contained.

'Shall we go? asked the girl.

She smiled at him in an engaging manner. Not finding anything to say in response, he stood up. The size of his body amazed him. He no longer had any defined outline. He was changing shape as he moved. "That's it, he thought sadly, I'm sloshed." On the floor, the mass of dancers refused to allow anyone to penetrate.

'We shall never be able to get in, he said.

'Yes, we will. You'll see. Through here. Look....A little space...Suddenly Etienne felt a warm body thrust itself against him, and his feet began to move with the rhythm. He was surrounded by bare and pale faces. The music had softened. Piano and bass drum. It was Marion who had taught him to dance, to the sound of an old, nasal gramophone, in front of the wardrobe with a mirror in the bedroom. At that time he was still wearing short trousers. But he was already as tall as his mother. He would hold her in his arms, awkwardly, his back arched, his neck stretched forward, moving forwards, backwards, turning to order, and she, smiling and proud, would keep time by moving her chin up and down: one, two...one, two...

'You're not that bad at dancing, said Yolande, but it's obvious that you're out of practice.

Her breath smelt of fruit pastilles. All her flesh, under her small, dark grey blouse, must be sweating.

'That's right, he said, I hardly ever dance.

'You don't like it?

'I don't have the time.

'Your studies?

'Yes.

She sighed:

'Your friends have told me that you're fantastic. Top in everything. I'm not surprised...

He was sensitive to this compliment and immediately hated his weakness. In the blink of an eye, he had forgotten that he despised the world. To strengthen his disdain, he inhaled deeply the smell of the men and of the women. Now, following M Thuillier's advice, he imagined, behind these envelopes of skin, heartburns, failed baccalaureats, urinary incontinence, debts of honour, jealousies, vices, fits of anger, deformities, all sorts of physical and moral decline, which rendered humanity execrable.

'I too would like to have pursued my studies, said Yolande, but I had to earn my living very early. How old do you think I am?

'I don't know..

'I'm twenty three. That's old! And yet, you see, I especially seek out the company of students. They're great, students, they're not afraid of living!

'Where did you get to know the Maroussels?

'At La Baule. they're great lads...

'Bloody idiots, said Etienne.

He had said these words without thinking, to satisfy a need to use bad language, to be violently concise.

'That's too strong, she said. What have you got against them?

'What I've got against them is that they sit when it's necessary to sit, and stand when it's necessary to stand.

'I don't understand.

'You can't understand.

'You mean that they lack personality?

'She was not as stupid as he had supposed on first impression.

'It's a bit like that, he murmured. They don't know how to assert themselves. They're nondescript, cautious. They live according to conventions that others have invented for them.

'And Biosque, Palaiseau, Kellermann?

'The same thing.

'And me?

He was embarrassed by this question, which he was not expecting, lost his thread, had to stop.

'And me? she continued, looking at him languorously through half closed eyelids.

Couples jostled them as they passed. He started dancing again, clumsily, his feet uncoordinated, his face burning.

'I don't know you well enough, he replied at last. I can't say.

'We shall see each other again, she whispered.

'If you like.

A degree of joy was mixed with his bitterness.

'Yes, I want to, she said, with sudden impudence. You interest me a good deal.

'Why?

'Because you're a strange one.

A black man jumped onto the stage and opened a huge mouth, big enough to crush an infant's skull. The skin of his face was thick, shiny, a greenish black colour, like a seal's. His teeth sparkled. He squealed. He sang. The rhythm was accelerating dangerously. Stricken with frenzy, all the puppets stomped up and down on the spot, obeying the wizard's commands.

'They have a lightning tempo, said Yolande, Can you follow?

Etienne nodded in agreement. The music and the whisky were combining in his stomach to produce a worryingly unreal sensation. Feeling sick, light headed, he was participating, body and soul, in the same activity as his neighbours. His legs were working independently of his will. It suddenly seemed that he understood the esoteric meaning of this din and of this agitation. It was not for the pleasure of dancing, that so many couples were thrashing about in an oven-like atmosphere. They were protesting in their own way against civilisation, such as old people had created it. They were challenging, by crazed gestures, the solemn and ossified universe in which their parents were condemning them to live. They were trampling, savagely, on a flowerbed of moral principles, of social superstitions, of outmoded national conventions. Yes, coming together in a cellar, like the first Christians, young people were affirming their desire for freedom, for disorder and risk. Etienne had been wrong in believing that they would hold his admission against him. To these people you could say everything. Having heard it, they would redouble their admiration for him. Yolande was pushing her stomach forward. Through the material of their clothes, their skins were becoming intimate. The black man roared:

'But ma-a-amy is gone.

She opened her lips. Etienne saw the inside of her mouth. He could have kissed her. The black man's face broke into pieces. The humming of a sewing machine emerged from his black throat. Etienne bent his face forward, met Yolande's intimate breath. His knees began to tremble. He said:

'I am the son of a murderer.

The band stopped playing. The silence of hell hovered over the dancers. Everyone had stopped, strings cut, arms hanging. The dance floor was emptying.

Yolande asked:

'What did you say?

Terrified by his lack of caution, Etienne murmured:

'Nothing, nothing...

'You did say something. I didn't hear with this din...

'I'm telling you again that I didn't say anything...

She screwed up her eyes. Her chest swelled, like a dove. Was she perhaps imagining that he had made a declaration of love? A whisper emerged from her lips:

'In the street it will be easier to talk.

He felt solid and dirty, cheerful and limp.

'Come, she said.

She was walking in front of him. Passing near the Maroussels' table, she shouted:

'We're going to get some air. Don't worry about us!

They replied with jeers. Paulette was sitting on the elder Maroussel's knees.

'We hope you enjoy yourselves! yelled Palaiseau.

After a pause, the band played a long, brassy groan. As at the sound of a factory siren, boys, girls, alive to their obligations, made their way to the dance floor. The staircase turned twice on itself before coming out on the level of the pavement. From the street the slight, muffled sounds of the music could still be heard. Etienne opened his mouth and swallowed a mouthful of fresh air. The lampposts kept watch, like candles, before the corpses of large middle class houses, with their sealed doors and closed shutters.

'You don't want to repeat what you said to me just now, whispered Yolande.

'No.

'It was so serious?

'Yes.

'And if I tried to guess?

'You wouldn't be able to.

'Oh! I'm very clever, she said.

The light from a lamppost lit up her face, fixed in an expression of indecent greed. She looked as if she were sniffing something nice.

'It was about us? she continued, quietly.

He did not have the courage to disappoint her.

'Yes, he said.

She shot him a radiant glance and declared in a whisper:

'I live very near here. Shall we go?

He wanted to reply but a feeling of languor tied his throat. Insects were running over his skin. His cowardice seemed, at one and the same time, both contemptible and useful. "I said what I had to say. Whether she heard or not, it makes no difference. From my own point of view, I'm in the right."

They walked a few steps, side by side. Then Yolande stopped, looked up, and Etienne pushed her against the wall of a house. His audacity and decisiveness amazed even himself. Never before had he imposed his will on a girl. And yet he was not embarrassed in his movements. Another person was within him.

'Oh! Yes, she said.

Their faces came together. He pressed his lips onto a bitter and wet mouth, which was opening. Suddenly, he felt alone no longer. In a delicious sensation Etienne felt that he and Yolande were as one. He was out of breath. "She loves me! I'm going to have a mistress! I'm happy!"

She moved away from him a little, her eyes bulging, leaning forward from the waist, as if she had stomach ache. People walked past them. She stammered:

'How tightly you held me in your arms! I thought you were going to kill me. You are strong. You are brutal. I like you...

He remained silent, overcome by the violence of his own desire. Fire was sweeping through his veins. His muscles were swelling. He wanted to bite, to strike, to force someone to kneel in the mud. Nothing would resist him. Everything was allowed. And for this power, he was indebted to his father.

Once again, he drew her against his chest.

'Darling! my darling! she groaned. We shall say nothing to the others. It will be our secret.

She was writhing. She was rubbing him with her belly. She was scratching his neck with her pointed fingernails. He thrust his face onto this large flower of chattering flesh. And suddenly a jolt of intense pleasure shook his bones. His head was bursting. His legs were becoming limp. He thought he was going to faint. He pushed her away.

'What's the matter, my darling?

Stunned, her eyes round, her lips bruised, she was looking at him, as if he had slapped her for no reason. Then she understood. Her face brightened:

'It's nothing. It happens. You wanted me too much. Let me carry on...

Her voice was horribly maternal. She came towards him, wanted to kiss him again. As if released from a magic spell, he endured with repugnance this deep and greedy kiss. M. Thuillier's words came back to him. These lips, this tongue, were the termination of eight metres of guts rolled into a ball. He was stuck to the orifice of a mass of connected intestines. He was breathing in the viscous interior of a woman who meant nothing to him. Horrified, he untied the two hands which were joined around his neck.

'No, he said, in a muffled voice. Clear off! Leave me alone!

He must have been frightening to see, for she lowered her shoulders, closed her eyes, shrank from her head to her feet.

Briskly, she turned her back on him and began running very quickly along the street. Her heels clattered on the asphalt.

When she was a long way off, he muttered:

'Bitch!

There was a sense of relief within him. The night, the houses, the sky, the lampposts, it was all given to him in exchange for the woman who had gone.

A little later, he noticed that he was walking in a street which must be the rue de la Seine. The sensation of his empty body was painful. He thought about the love extolled by the poets, and which, all things considered, was only a despicable passion, seeing that a physical accident could transform desire into disgust. What illusion were men and women under, celebrating like a miracle the most shameful manifestations of their glands? Why was this natural function surrounded by more consideration than the one they satisfied every day in the toilet? An additional lie, invented by honest people, to conceal the disgrace of their condition. Behind the everlasting vows, the swooning glances, the lipstick, the perfumes, the élans of the soul, there were only mucous spasms. Everything was dirty in the world. Dirty and ugly. You only had to look at people to understand that God did not exist. Indeed, could one conceive that an all powerful creator had made a mess of his work to such an extent? Did one have to adore a principle which heaped up intrinsic miseries, inequality of races, differences in fortunes and talents, disease, death, the ridiculous variability of possession?

Suddenly he regretted not having followed Yolande into her bedroom. In order to demean himself further. To know exactly what this penetration of one sexual organ into another was. In order to proclaim his hatred, his scorn, before a body naked and gratified. She had been afraid of him. She had fled, as if he had threatened her with a gun. He wondered if he would have been capable of killing her, in a fit of anger. Thrusting his hand into his pocket, he took out the photograph. Indisputably, he resembled his father. The square of newsprint trembled between his fingers. He put the picture away in his wallet. Why did this comparison with Louis Martin have to be limited to facial features? From one generation to another, moral heredity played as strong a role as physical heredity. A father, a mother passed on to their child not only a particular external form, but also their most violent and secret instincts. It did not depend on Etienne that his heredity should be rich or poor, that his bone structure should develop in this way or that. Similarly, he could not be held responsible for the feelings which were going around in his soul. The mystery of his destiny, like the shape of his nose, was contained in the productive cells which had come together in the insemination between his parents.

The void, the darkness into which he was rapidly sinking, were assisting him in this glorious conviction. Hot fury was building in his hands. His eyes were no longer alighting on objects, but were striking them, as if to open them. As an indirect consequence, he was experiencing a slight hollow pain in his eye socket. "Marked out for evil, from my birth, it is this evening that I am waking up to my condition. Louis Martin was no doubt like me, for many years a young man proper and nondescript. And suddenly he felt this need, this power come to life within him. In my turn, they now come to me. At that time, courageously, he accepted that he would play the role, which had devolved onto him. He assumed the terrible vocation, which, this day, through the marrying of creative cells, is becoming mine. And the law of men punished him because he obeyed the law of nature."

Rue Visconti. A silent tunnel, bordered by facades. Two cars passed, one towing the other. The double headed silhouette of a couple entered the front of a house. A moonbeam softened the angle of the rue Bonaparte. Etienne jumped. Right next to him, a small, grey cat, with fur standing on end and tail upright, was miaowing in front of a black wooden door, which refused to open. "And him, could I kill him?" he wondered. A feeling of urgency made the hairs on the back of his neck stand on edge. He crouched down and clicked his tongue discreetly. The animal came to rub himself against his knees. Two round eyes, the colour of phosphorous. A tiny mouth with high-pitched squeals. Still too young to be timid. Etienne picked him up, pressed him against his chest. The kitten flattened his ears and purred with contentment. Gradually, Etienne's hand penetrated this tuft of warm fur. He felt the life of another creature throbbing lightly under his fingers. "A sharp blow on the spine and it will be all over. Delicate vertebrae, soft belly, velvety paws. I am undertaking my apprenticeship on a cat. Come on, have some courage. Louis Martin would not have hesitated." He stood up. A gloomy feeling of anguish came over him. He was panting, coming to grips with a redoubtable enemy, which weighed as little as a ball of wool. He gathered all his strength, all his will, against this inconspicuous soul. A policeman passed by, pedalling calmly on his bicycle, with its light bouncing up an down. Etienne opened his hands. The cat fell on the pavement and shot away, flat to the ground, furtive.

"I didn't dare. Or rather, I didn't have the time. Later, later..." He set off again, dragging the souls of his shoes, his mouth open, like a thirsty man. Stone after stone, window after window, still more houses, asleep and with food in their bellies. In the distance, the lights of the Saint-Germain-des-Pres crossroads were shining. Two men and a woman sprang from the darkness. They were laughing and talking. No mystery for them. Proud of their indifferent looks and happy after an excellent evening, which had only cost 895 francs, service included. Etienne imagined them lying on the pavement, their skulls smashed, their faces smeared with a mess of fresh blood. This image caused him no concern at all. He did not see why he had to value these unknown people on the grounds that they had, like him, a head, two arms and two legs. "If I wring the neck of a cat, nobody will say anything; if I strangle a woman, I shall be a criminal of the worst sort. I am free to hate spiders, but not to hate my fellow human beings. No-one can force me to like a dish of cod à la provençale, but everybody wants me to like people. And who is responsible for this absurdity?"

He had stopped in front of the window of a shop selling religious trinkets.

'Him, he said quietly. Him alone. This statue!...

Nausea, tasting of whisky, filled his mouth. He swallowed his saliva, shrugged his shoulders and turned away from the darkened window.

The last metro train having gone, he had to return home on foot. The avenue de Tourville belonged to a provincial town, muffled, distant, friend of trees, sleep and good behaviour. Exhausted, his shoes burning and his legs weak, Etienne made slow progress, alone, under the thick foliage which hid the sky. Gradually, his drunkenness had dissipated. When he reflected on the events of the evening, he felt confused, and doubted that he had actually experienced them. The greedy woman, the cat, people out walking, the black man in the band, for him were part of a nightmare with characters he could not believe in.

He regretted his misadventure with Yolande. What did she think of him now? Would she agree to see him again, after what had happened? He dreamed of new embraces, no longer grotesque, but wild, touching, sublime. Yolande becoming his mistress. An unknown bedroom shielding their love. His friends envying him. "Tomorrow everything will be simpler. I can't take alcohol. My mind wanders." He felt very young, very vulnerable. A lost child, An orphan. He desperately wanted to return to his bed, his books, the friendship of the furniture and the walls. Already he could make out the end of his long walk: a house of seven stories, like the rest, and which was only important because it was his house.

Suddenly he stopped, as if suffering an electric shock. Fifteen metres from him, outside the front door, a woman and a man held each other in an embrace. Marion! The stocky build of the unknown man hid her, partly absorbed her. Leaning over her, it was obvious that he was passionately kissing her mouth. A shiver of horror seized Etienne's heart and spread out, like a fan, to the extremities of his body. Never before had he imagined what Marion's meetings with Maxime Joubert could be like. For him, their relationship existed in the centre of an abstract region. And suddenly here they were, these two people, entering his field of vision, with their caresses, which were just like everybody else's. Marion was pressing her body against her lover, as Yolande had pressed herself against Etienne, with the same shamelessness, the same frenzy. And Maxime Joubert, standing stiffly in front of his mistress, was experiencing, in this moment, the same intimate jubilation which Etienne had known, thanks to another woman. "A disgusting farce. Filth. And Marion is participating in the vile pleasures of the flesh!" The shadows separated. Etienne would like to have died on the spot. But life held onto him.

"Men of my sort do not use their will to die, but to kill. I am not a candidate for suicide, but for murder. I have a murderer's blood in my veins. Don't forget it." Over there a man was bowing in front of a woman, was gallantly kissing her hand. Gentle words were being exchanged in the kindly night. "I love you. Until tomorrow. A whole day without you!" Two hearts were beating rapidly. A crumpled petticoat. Damp trousers. That was what love was.

Etienne licked his lips which were impregnated with a taste of make up and alcohol. The front door opened. Marion spun round, disappeared. Maxime Joubert waited a few seconds more in front of the closed door. He looked as if he were following, as if he could see through wood, the passage of the young woman into the entrance hall of the house. Then he made his way slowly to the kerb. A car, low to the ground and black, was parked there, under a lamppost. Frowning, opening wide his eyes, Etienne was trying to make out, from a distance, the features of this happy man. He observed that he was close shaven, and he noticed his grey hair and the white flash of his false collar. A car door shut. Headlights shone out. Afraid of being seen, Etienne pressed himself against a tree trunk. The car slipped away in front of him and insulted him, as it went by, with the sparkle of expensive engineering. It was over. He was alone. But he no longer dared to approach the front door.

For a long time he walked around in the neighbouring streets, with his hands in his pockets and an evil expression on his face. It was three o'clock in the morning when he at last decided to go home. In the dark apartment the furniture was sleeping on its feet. No trace of light under Marion's door; she was resting, exhausted by an excess of a lover's tiredness. Certainly she had not felt the need to check if her son had returned from his walk. She was sure of him: "A responsible boy. Let's go to bed without waking him. It's late. I am the happiest of women." Maxime Joubert was occupying her dreams and regulating her breathing. The small clock on the mantelpiece chimed, in the darkness, with a clear, hollow ring. One of the floor tiles creaked. Etienne took off his shoes and made his way to his bedroom, walking on tiptoe.

Chapter Ten

Etienne was finishing his breakfast when his mother came into the kitchen. She had got up late and still seemed sleepy.

'Marthe and Suzanne are already here, she said. And me dillydallying. It's irresponsible! Quickly, a cup of hot coffee!

While speaking she held out her cheek to her son for the ritual morning kiss. He stood up and touched, with the extremity of his lips and with extreme caution, this cool skin, which smelled of almond scented beauty cream. Contrary to what he expected, this initial contact raised no repugnance within him. He had difficulty in believing that this modest and gentle person, seated opposite him, had swooned, the evening before, in the arms of a man. Observing her surreptitiously, he was looking for physical signs of degradation, and could only see a calm and familiar face, two clear eyes, the everyday smile. He sat down again and carried on eating.

'I hope I didn't wake you up when I came back yesterday evening, she continued. It was so late!

'I didn't hear anything, he said.

'That's what I thought.

She was pouring the coffee and the milk, buttering a slice of bread, and he avoided looking up, for fear that she would notice the worried expression on his face. How could she be, by turns, and with equal conviction, female creature and woman, mistress and mother? He would like to have condemned her without mercy. But, from one day to the next, one person had been substituted for another. The accused of the day before was no longer there. Somebody else was taking her place.

'You had a good evening with M Maxime Joubert? he asked in a falsely casual tone.

'Excellent. We dined at the Tour d'Argent. And from there we went to a cabaret in Montmartre.

'The comedians were funny?

'Extremely funny, Etienne! I really laughed...

"She laughed. While I was suffering like a condemned man. And, coming back from the show, she gave her body to a man who had paid for her to eat and drink." He was ashamed for Marion and for himself, at the heartbreaking turn events were taking. Filthy trickles of water were running into him, through a thousand pin holes. He was suffocating: "It's not possible. She's not like the others. She will pull herself together. This Maxime Joubert will not mean anything to her. He will pass. And we shall remain the two of us, she and I. In Louis Martin's shadow."

'And what did you do, my darling?

He wanted to rush to embrace her, cover her with kisses, tell her that he had seen everything and that she was wrong to behave with this shameful flightiness. But his concern about a sense of propriety kept him in his place. He was afraid that such an admission would forever compromise their relationship. For some days he had no longer been able to speak to her with the same frankness as before. Formerly they had been friends who had no secrets from each other. Now they lived separately, in different spheres, he thinking about a dead man, and she a living one. Suppressing his tenderness, his need, he said:

'I ate with some friends

'Is that all?

'No. Afterwards we met up at Fisto. It's a nightclub.

'And you danced?

She was smiling gently. She had an ironic and affectionate expression. He realised, with some bitterness, that she persisted in considering him a child.

'Why wouldn't I dance? he said sharply.

'It's hardly something you normally do...

She finished her coffee and asked again:

'So there were girls with you?

'Obviously.

'What kind of girls?

'Girls like all girls, mum.

She sighed:

'Alright, alright...

He found it odd that she should be so punctilious when it concerned people her son mixed with, and so careless when it was a question of those she mixed with herself. Had she forgotten the taste of that man's mouth on her mouth, the weight of those masculine hands on her back?

'Still, she said, you shouldn't take it into your head to go out like that with friends every evening...

'If you had stayed at home, I wouldn't have had the idea of going out enjoying myself elsewhere, he replied in a brusque manner.

She looked at him sadly. And, immediately, he regretted his words. He felt a sense of panic.

'You hold that against me? she asked.

'Of course not, mum.

Marion got up and carried the cups to the sink. Rain was coming in through the open window. A few breadcrumbs lay on the red and white waxed tablecloth. Etienne wiped them off with the back of his hand. He looked at his mother from behind. A girl's shoulder blades under a sweater of fine black wool. A pleated skirt. Slippers of maroon satin, with heels slightly at an angle. "How small she is! How obviously she belongs to me! Helpless, unknowing, frivolous. I must protect her." Suddenly, she turned towards him and, with half a smile, said:

'I've invited M Maxime Joubert to dinner this evening.

He was expecting anything but this news. The surprise left him weak at the knees. A bomb had just burst into this nondescript decor of tiles and saucepans. Mastering his inner turmoil, he stammered:

'Ah! Really? That's very good.

Seconds were passing and he continued to tremble throughout his body. How did she dare bring this individual into the house? Were there no other places in Paris to shield their amorous liaisons?

'We shall be ready to eat at about half past eight, she went on.

He made an effort to speak. His face felt painful, as if he had received a slap:

'Fine. I shall go out about that time, to leave you to it.

She frowned:

'Are you mad?

'Not at all. My presence would embarrass you, I'm sure.

As if overcome by dizziness, she closed her eyes for a moment. She sucked her cheeks in. Then she opened her eyelids again and said firmly:

'M Maxime Joubert is a friend whom I hold in high esteem. You must get to know him.

'What's the point? I don't interest him. And I doubt that he will interest me.

'You are wrong to think that, Etienne. If I am insisting that you meet him, it's because I have a reason.

'I don't deny it.

'I've often spoken to him about you...

'And you've often spoken to me about him. We're quits.

'Don't be stubborn, Etienne.

'I'm sorry, but you will do without me. That will be better for everybody.

She was struggling to master the fury which shone through her whole being. Suddenly she shouted:

'That's enough, Etienne! Your fit of bad temper is ridiculous. I demand that you eat with us this evening. And that you are pleasant to our guest. Later, if you persist in your opinion, I will not ask you to see M Maxime Joubert again. But you must know people before judging them. You are still a kid. You are being awkward. And I am too weak with you, I let you say...

Dumbfounded, dismayed, Etienne put up with this outburst of feminine anger. Never before had his mother spoken to him in this hostile manner. Captivated by Maxime Joubert, she now saw in her son only an obstacle to her pitiful, late flowering love. She was sacrificing eighteen years of affection, of confidences, of mutual protection, to the vulgar desire of a greying, lecherous man.

'I hope you have understood, she continued.

'Yes, I have understood, mum, he said quietly.

'I can rely on you?

'Rely on me. Understood. I shall stay...

He was amazed that he was suffering so greatly and that he felt so alone.

The sewing machine, which had not been working all morning, emitted its monotonous humming. A tap, not properly turned off, was dripping steadily onto the washing up piled in the bowl in the sink.

'Thank you, my darling, whispered Marion.

And she left the kitchen.

Alone, he no longer felt at ease with his sorrow. "She no longer loves me. She prefers this newcomer, this swine. She cannot guess that she is preparing our unhappiness, for both of us, by behaving like this."

He got up, went over to the window. A little of the grey sky could be seen between the roofs. The temperature was mild. No doubt there would soon be rain. Marion did not have the right, at her age and in her position, to behave like a kid deprived of caresses. By throwing herself at this Maxime Joubert she was renouncing her past and compromising her future. She was devoting her body and soul to an individual, whose sole merit consisted in being alive, the very type of those old people who govern the world according to outmoded conceptions. "It's with *that* that she deceives Louis Martin, it's with *that* that she does not hesitate to turn my life upside down. Here, I am in my own home. Let her meet someone else outside: fine! But not between these walls, not in front of this table, which has always brought us together, face to face, at meal times." Suddenly, he thought that he would not be alone, this evening, suffering the insult of an undesirable presence. Sole heir of his father, possessor of his name, of his secret, of his blood, he had a mission to defend, in the face of everyone and against everyone, the interest of this inglorious dead man. It was Louis Martin, who delegated him, at Marion's side, to prevent her committing a serious misdemeanour. Charged with this order, could he welcome favourably the man who was encouraging Louis Martin's widow to forget her first marriage? Was he to make himself the accomplice of this posthumous betrayal?

He saw himself sitting between his mother and his mother's lover, he, the son of a murderer, listening to their trifling conversation, smiling, passing the bread, pouring the wine, being charming so that this newcomer might feel confident in the house. "However insane this might appear, she expects nothing else from me. She wants me to seduce him in my turn. She wants me to remove her last scruples!" His memory was mixing the present and the past. When he still did not know that his father was a murderer, his indulgence towards Marion was total. He did not suffer when he saw that she was in love with another man. It seemed to him that he encouraged her, even, to find pleasure in the company of Maxime Joubert. Today this very thought was intolerable. The ignominious death of Louis Martin gave him rights over his widow, over his son, over the entire universe. After what men had done to him, he deserved more pity than ordinary dead people. He existed apart, on a throne of blood, in the innumerable crowd of the deceased. Drops of rain struck against the window ledge.

Etienne took a step back in the room. "That's settled. I shall not stay for this grotesque dinner. Without saying anything to Marion, I shall leave the house and only return late into the night. They will do what they like in my absence."

By a strange quirk of imagination, he saw himself, hair blowing in the wind, walking in the dark streets of the neighbourhood. Several times he walked past the solid and austere block of flats in the avenue de Tourville, looked up at the windows. Behind the lighted glass panes Marion and Maxime Joubert continued their lovers' tea party. Champagne and foie gras, brief kisses and hands touching under the table. Meanwhile, he, driven from the family home, wandered in the darkness, like a beggar, like an outlaw. "When they have eaten well and drunk well, she will show him my bedroom. He shall see my butterflies, my plaster bust, my books. He will smell my aroma and walk over my floor. Then she shall take him into her room, with impatient laughter, fluttering her eyelids. He will put his trousers on the chair where I usually sit. He will sleep with her in the bed where I have always seen her on her own."

For a few seconds he believed that this wretched scene was real. The night genuinely surrounded him. And there was a bright window in the depths of his brain. He understood, with despair, that it would be as difficult for him to flee the house as to stay. Here, as elsewhere, at the table as in the street, he was condemned to futile suffering. This man was turning him out from his rightful place. There was no longer any room for him in the world. Oh! if only Maxime Joubert could have died, disappeared. An illness, a car accident. But people like him were indestructible. "He will be there at the agreed time, clean shaven, all dressed up, with his professional smile and his hand extended."

Carried along by a kind of intoxication, Etienne began to whisper swearwords, seeking in his heart the terms best chosen to wound the couple. His lips were twisting themselves around filthy words. He had to stop himself from shouting them out.

After a moment, he stopped, exhausted by the petty slave-like revolt. "If Louis Martin had been in my place, he would not have been content to offer insults. He would have taken responsibility and acted, and risked everything. He would have gone to Maxime Joubert's house to settle the matter. A gunshot. Finished. Nobody there any more."

A sharp joy pierced his heart. The outline of the objects around him became blurred in a coal black mist. In the depths of this fog saucepans were gleaming like silver moons. Slowly, with a feigned calm, Etienne made his way towards the door.

Walking past the dining room, he heard the women chatting. But his ears registered their remarks only as a murmur from a far off valley. Gradually, solemnly, he found the refuge of his bedroom, darkened and refreshed by the rain which was falling heavily. On the table lay part of a work by Schopenhauer, *The world as will and as representation*. He only had volume three of this work, purchased some while ago on the quays, where he happened to be walking. Etienne leafed through the book to find a passage that he had recently read. Page 328:

> By coming together in the act of generating life, the seed carried by the parents reproduce not only the characteristics of the species, but also those of individuals...Let each person begin by considering himself, his preferences and his passions...Let him then think back to his father, and he will not fail to notice in him these character traits as a whole; the mother, on the other hand, will often be of a very different character and a moral convergence with her will be one of the rarest phenomena...

Further on came a series of historic examples, intended to prove that, from father to son, the same vices and the same virtues were in operation in the world. Tiberius, Caligula, Nero, the Borgias[1].

> In the month of October 1836, in Hungary, Count Belezcnai was condemned to death for murdering a civil servant and seriously wounding his own parents...His father had also been guilty of murder...

Etienne smiled, nodded and carried on reading. A clear spell of weather was, in his mind, succeeding the storm which had assailed him at first. He felt, with delight, that his own will was weakening, absorbed into the will of another. Second by second, he was ceding more space to the new being who was developing within him and who was ridding him of his last fears. He remained like this, leaning over his table, leafing through the old book with its green cover, until the time when Marion called him for lunch.

They ate in silence, sitting opposite each other, in the room where the everyday noise of the street penetrated. Marion had the pale and wounded face of a convalescent. She was breathing rapidly through her nose. But Etienne could not feel sorry for her. She could not suspect that she was sitting in front of Louis Martin. When she looked up it was Louis Martin she saw, without knowing it. If she decided to speak, it would be Louis Martin to whom her words would be addressed. He recited to himself, mentally, the line of Shakespeare, quoted by Schopenhauer: 'Cowards beget cowards, and from baseness is born baseness.'

The cleaning lady came to clear the table. Then, Mme Marthe and Mlle Suzanne filled the house with their cackling of happy hens. Etienne went back to his bedroom. At five o'clock in the afternoon he heard Marion go out. No doubt she was going to do the shopping for dinner. Nothing would be too good to celebrate the entrance of Maxime Joubert into the family.

Etienne waited twenty more minutes, then slipped, like a shadow, into the hall. The telephone directory stood on the chest next to the coat rack. He opened the volume and moved to the glass door, which let in the light. Once again, women's voices, the noise of a sewing machine, haunting, annoying:

'Pass me the chalk, Suzanne.

A pair of scissors fell onto the floor. "Joubert M. 17, rue de La Trémoille". Etienne put the directory back in its place and pushed open the door which led to his mother's bedroom. Maxime Joubert's roses were still there, the stems shortened, the petals faded. The perfume of dead flowers hung in the room, which was empty and clean, where it seemed that nobody had ever lived. Walking on tiptoe, Etienne moved towards the bedside table and placed his hand on the yellowing sycamore ball which served as a handle. The drawer creaked open. Black and clean, the revolver lay in the bottom of its case.

*

The housekeeper, with her lined and weather beaten face, observed Etienne kindly.

'Monsieur never returns from the office before six o'clock, she said. Do you have an appointment?

'Yes, said Etienne.

'In that case, perhaps you could wait for him. I shall show you in.'

She smiled at him. She no doubt judged him to have good manners and an honest face.

'If you would like to follow me...'

She crossed the hall, with its cold stone floor. It was adorned by an ancient chest, dotted with studs, and a single picture, very large and very dark, representing a Jesuit at prayer. A huge door, with a pattern carved in the shape of a diamond, turned on its hinges and Etienne entered a low room lined with many books and much wood panelling.

'Monsieur will not be long, said the housekeeper.

The door closed noiselessly. Etienne remained standing, intimidated by the studious and sober order of the surroundings. Guided by an intrinsic dislike, he had imagined that Maxime Joubert lived in a spacious interior in poor taste, full of furniture with offensive gilding. At the present time he was finding it difficult to believe that this person, whom he hated yet did not know, had conceived and created such an attractive home. Between two arched windows, with small panes, was spread a green and dark brown tapestry, depicting a wood at dusk. On the long table, of polished cherry wood, there were paperback books, newspapers, an inkwell in black stone. In an ashtray lay two pipes, one straight and the other curved. There was an aroma of tobacco in the air. "He smokes a pipe. I didn't know. Anyway, what difference does that make?" Etienne went over to the shelves laden with books: "Chateaubriand[2], Daudet[3], Anatole France[4]. Obviously, it goes with his age. Ah! all the same, a Baudelaire[5], a Rimbaud[6]. *Les Chants de Maldoror.* Has he even read them?" Suddenly his heart gave a start, failed him: Schopenhauer, *The world as will and as representation.* The three volumes. He took the first volume of the series. The pages had been cut with care[7]. Here and there, sentences underlined in pencil. He read a few words:

> The more the will is violent and the more it multiplies its efforts,
> the more violent and numerous will be the sufferings that it causes as
> a consequence...What I regret is not what I have willed, but what I have
> done...

Etienne replaced the volume in the row and pushed it back into its place. Next to it were the works of Spinoza[8], Freud[9], Leibniz[10], Plato. Etienne's eyes took in this company of illustrious names, He had never supposed that Maxime Joubert, a dealer in textiles, would have read works of such remarkable quality. This discovery was modifying the idea that he had conceived of his opponent. It seemed to him that, at the last moment, a treacherous hand had changed the target on which his attention was fixed. The man he was going to kill was not just a nondescript individual, but a lover of philosophy, a reader of Schopenhauer. "And so what? Am I going to forgive him, on account of his not being a complete ignoramus? What have my intellectual preferences got to do with a debate like this?" However, his unease was growing and he was irritated with himself for not being able to diminish it. He could almost have reproached Maxime Joubert for unnecessarily complicating the task.

Turning his back on the bookshelves, he chose a leather armchair, sat down, felt in his pocket the butt of the revolver which had become warm by rubbing, through the lining, against his skin. Contact with this gun, always at the ready, increased, at one and the same time, his self assurance and his sense of fright. "The power of objects over people. Without the revolver I am nothing. With a revolver, I become the master of life and death. The revolver is a key to understanding the world. Just a pity that I've got to do it here. Here, I am a visitor. You must behave properly in other people's houses. Not make a noise. Not make anything dirty. Everything is so clean! So tidy! There will be blood. A large, dark stain on the carpet. Will it come out when it's cleaned? I shall apologise, as if I had spilled some wine. But, at my feet, the body, broken, pierced, will not wish to hear anything. He will look at me, with his big white eyes, reproachfully, because I will have made his carpet dirty. And he will be right. But what can I do? Impossible not to kill, at the same time, both the setting and the one who lives within it."

Etienne sighed and considered with distress the books, the pipes, the lamp, the curtains, all these objects which were aware of his decision and which were awaiting the arrival of the main actor at the place of execution. The silence and the emptiness of the room made him realise that he had never been so close to carrying out his plan. A quarter of an hour, half an hour at most, separated him from the death of Maxime Joubert. This prospect gave him no joy, but was no less exciting for that. He only had to think of Louis Martin to know that his own hand would not tremble at the moment chosen for the sacrifice. He was now keeping his fingers on the revolver, which was becoming damp with sweat. In order to accustom himself to the idea of committing murder, he was imagining the noise of the gun firing, the body falling clumsily, the piercing cries of the housekeeper. He was saying to himself: "By my decision alone, what has been will be no longer. My action will make me a murderer and make him a corpse. Now, every act is honourable in itself. As Thuillier states, there are no men who are guilty, only those who are responsible. Schopenhauer is responsible for a book and I shall be responsible for a murder. When he learns what has happened, my teacher will be proud of me."

Suddenly he wondered what would happen to him after his arrest. which was already certain. A prison cell, judgement, death. "Like my father." Admirable logic of this heredity from one generation to another. The delight of total resemblance in brutality and despair. Pride in the name, in the blood, in the vocation passed on and accepted. "Inner turmoil worthy of a king!" But perhaps he would not be guillotined? He was not old enough. No punishment frightened him. He found himself in a situation where there was no way out. Surrounded, suffocated, he had, under pain of asphyxiation, to smash down this living rampart. He looked at Louis Martin's watch on his wrist. Five past six. "What is he waiting for?" A fit of impatience gripped him, as if he had arranged a meeting with Maxime Joubert and the latter's lateness was unforgiveable.

Exasperated, he got up, walked around the room, where his steps, absorbed by the beige carpet, created no echo. He noticed a photograph in a marquetry frame standing on the work table. Contrary to what he had thought, the picture was not of Marion, but an old lady with a white bun and the lines of wisdom in her face. Maxime Joubert's mother perhaps. As far as Marion was concerned, her picture was no doubt hidden in a locked drawer somewhere. "He opens the drawer and he looks at her. He picks up the 'phone and speaks to her. He makes use of her like an object." At this very thought a renewal of anger enflamed him. The murderous power, this sort of gift which he had inherited from his father, was rising into his muscles, running under his skin, like a stimulating, joyful electric current. He was trembling from his head to his toes, like a runner at the start of a race. "Quick! Let him come! Let's get it over with! I've had enough of waiting!" Several seconds passed in total silence. Life seemed suspended, so profound was the stillness of everything.

Etienne took out his revolver, weighed it in his hand, put it back in his pocket. In its frame of varnished wood, an old lady, with her lined face and white hair, watched his every gesture. A fit of dizziness blurred Etienne's thoughts. He closed his eyes. At that precise moment, in the depths of the flat, a door closed, a voice could be heard. Etienne started and looked up. A solemn dread swelled his chest. "There is no doubt. It's him. He's talking with the servant. He's reproaching her for showing me in, without asking my name. He's coming. And what am I going to do? I shall only fire when I have spoken to him. Tell him everything before killing him like a dog. Oh! God, give me the strength..."

Now, turning towards the carved door, he was listening, stupefied, intoxicated, to the steps of this man he did not know, who was advancing, with heavy tread, towards death.

The door opened to admit a man of average build, with a pale face, and wearing a grey suit. Nothing in common, it seemed, with the person who, the previous night, had kissed Marion in the doorway. Seen from a distance, the other seemed well built.

This one was rather slim, with a tired and gentle look, a high forehead, hair streaked with grey and swept back. Disconcerted, Etienne contemplated this fraudulent stand-in for Maxime Joubert, who was closing the door and walking straight towards the desk.

'My apologies, said the man, but I have just learned that you have been waiting for me for a long while. As I do not have the honour of knowing you...

'I am Etienne Martin, murmured Etienne.

Maxime Joubert's face relaxed into a smile:

'Goodness me! I wasn't counting on making your acquaintance before this evening...

He held out his hand. Etienne let go the revolver which he was gripping deep in his pocket. His fingers emerged into the fresh air and met the fingers of Maxime Joubert.

With a degree of shame, he felt, in the joints of his fingers, this manly pressure, this promise of openness and friendship, coming from a man he had resolved to kill.

'Has your mother sent you? asked Maxime Joubert, pointing to an armchair.

He himself sat behind the table and began to scrape out a pipe. Etienne remained standing.

'No, he said.

'She doesn't know you are here?

Maxime Joubert seemed surprised. An indication of concern could be seen in his clear eyes, with their puckered eyelids. His eyebrows met. He replaced the pipe in the ashtray. As Etienne remained silent, he went on in a more serious tone:

'You shouldn't have come. Your mother was greatly looking forward to introducing us during dinner. By forestalling her plans, you are depriving her of a pleasure which she had been counting on for some weeks.

Etienne's throat was becoming dry. He swallowed a trickle of saliva and declared harshly:

'It was essential. I had to speak to you...

And, once again, he thrust his hand into his pocket. The presence of the revolver had the effect of calling him to order. Maxime Joubert asked:

'What do you want to speak to me about?

'About you, about my mother, about me.

'I understand, said Maxime Joubert.

A brief, sad grimace caused the corners of his lips to drop. He looked older, and agreeable.

'What are your intentions? uttered Etienne in a hoarse voice.

'Good gracious, said Maxime Joubert, it's an interrogation.

'Yes, said Etienne.

'Well, my intentions are very simple. I want to marry your mother. I have told her. And she has asked me to wait.

'Why?

'Because she was afraid of your reaction. I know from her that you are a generous, anxious, passionate young man and that we mustn't ride roughshod over your feelings...

Etienne clenched his jaws with loathing. Why had Marion said so much about him to this man? Disgusting conceit of mothers. A feminine tendency for gossip and indiscretion.

No doubt the better to captivate the person to whom she was speaking, she had exaggerated her son's qualities, presenting him as an extraordinary being, top in everything, sensitive to everything, and of no earthly use to anyone. Now, Maxime Joubert was comparing the fiction with reality. His eyes were fixed on Etienne, as on a book. He was deciphering a confused text. After a brief pause, he went on:

'Let me put myself in your position. Having lived alone with your mother for many years, it is natural that you should be annoyed at the thought of the change which this marriage will bring to your life. First of all, you consider me to be an intruder. I suppose, even, that I must seem to you to be disagreeable.

'You are not mistaken, monsieur, stammered Etienne.

And he blushed at his insolence. He did not like to be disrespectful to someone older than himself. "What does that matter, since I'm going to kill him?" Maxime Joubert leaned back in his chair.

'Thank you for being frank, he said. And I hope that, gradually, you will change your opinion. When you know me better, you will understand that you have been wrong to treat me like an enemy.

'I don't want to know you better.

'Why? There is nothing remarkable about me. But I believe that we could live on good terms. In many respects, my interests are the same as yours.

'This evening's dinner was meant to placate me? You would have spoken about art and philosophy in order to win my confidence. ..

'I would have done my best to bring about between us a friendly understanding which your mother desires with all her heart.

'This understanding is impossible! cried Etienne. I forbid you to marry my mother!

There was a silence. Maxime Joubert crossed his hands and placed them on the edge of the table. His features tightened. Anger flashed in his eyes.

'By what right, if you please, do you intend to forbid us from marrying? he said in a voice which was trembling slightly.

Etienne struggled for breath. His knees were buckling under the weight of his body. Gathering all his energy, he stammered:

'You don't know...You don't know who I am, who we are...

'Yes, I do, said Maxime Joubert. You are the son of Louis Martin, who was executed for murder.

Overwhelmed, his face lifeless, his eyes bulging, Etienne whispered:

'She's told you?

'Yes.

'She dared to tell you?...

This revelation frightened him, like the declaration of something sacrilegious. By admitting her secret to Maxime Joubert, Marion had desecrated Louis Martin's memory. She had allowed a stranger, alive, in good health, well-to-do, to judge and denigrate the man who had died at the guillotine. She had sought, for herself, the compassion of an additional member of the jury. "It's mean, it's shameful. Never shall I forgive her for her fecklessness", thought Etienne. Wild rage consumed him, forced him to look away.

'I can imagine what she might have told you about him, he said very aggressively. But what amazes me is to see that, despite the information she's given you, you are willing to take the place of a murderer at her side.

'How is your mother responsible for the atrocities committed by her husband? Her ill luck, her self sacrifice renders her all the more precious in my eyes.

'When did she have ill luck? When did she give proof of self sacrifice? muttered Etienne.

Saliva rose to his lips.

'Your mother, said Maxime Joubert, lived through terrible days at the time of the trial. She has struggled courageously to forget that horror, to bring you up in a worthy manner, to make of you, in opposition to your father, a respected, well educated man...

'I forbid you to insult my father! shouted Etienne.

'I'm not insulting him. I am merely stating the facts. He has several crimes on his conscience, and I think that you will agree with me...

'Be quiet!...You cannot understand...You forget that I am his flesh and blood, that I am his heir, that I represent him...

His tongue tripped over his words. There was a sensation of dizziness before his eyes.

'So you are not frightened to have, as a stepson, the actual son of Louis Martin? he continued, panting. And what if I were like him, if I resembled him?

'You are not remotely like your father, said Maxime Joubert coldly.

'What do you know about it? yelped Etienne.

He drew the revolver from his pocket. Maxime Joubert moved back sharply. His cheeks lost their colour. His eyes became fixed and hard.

'What do you want from me? he said at last.

'I have come to kill you, murmured Etienne. Maxime Joubert reached towards his pipe.

'Don't move! shouted Etienne.

And he thought: "Exactly as in the films." The hand, docile, returned to its place. There was silence between the two men. Against the skin of his fingers, Etienne felt the pure solidity of the gun, ready to explode, to deliver death. The knowledge of the power seemed exhilarating. He was aiming at Maxime Joubert and was telling himself that this person, greying, experienced, wearing an expensive flannel suit and surrounded by valuable books, existed only in so far as he, Etienne, allowed him to carry on living. Louis Martin must have felt the same exultation in front of his victims, pale with fright. "I have him at my mercy. He is no longer thinking of Marion, but of his precious little body, which, any moment now, will have given up its final sigh."

'Why are you waiting to shoot? asked Maxime Joubert.

'That's my business, said Etienne.

He was taking great pleasure in prolonging the game. He guessed that, behind his back, someone strong and competent was declaring himself to be satisfied with him. His finger was becoming numb on the trigger. the barrel of the gun was moving imperceptibly. At the end of his line of sight there was this corpse in preparation. Suddenly, Etienne noticed that Maxime Joubert had a scar on his left cheek. A pale furrow marked the flesh beneath the cheekbone. War wound? Which war? '14 or '39? With blokes of that age you couldn't tell! Etienne was unsettled by the scar. It seemed that it would have been easier, cleaner, to kill a man whose skin was intact. As if speaking to himself, he muttered:

'I shall kill you when I want.

'I don't doubt it, said Maxime Joubert, but allow me to point out that your attitude is based on a miscalculation.

He wanted to appear calm. Yet his face was quivering with agitation. Gradually, his eyes were widening, darkening. like those of a hypnotist.

'I'm not thinking of myself when I tell you that, he went on, but of yourself and of your mother. After my death, you will be arrested, judged, condemned to prison for many years. And so you will have compromised your whole future for the relatively minor pleasure of placing a bullet in my flesh. As for your mother, she who has suffered so much through having had a murderer for a husband, how will she feel when she learns that her son, in his turn, has been guilty of a murder?

Maxime Joubert's eyes widened further. Caught in their orbit, Etienne was giving way to the effects of a pleasant fascination. "This time I shall fire", he thought. But his index finger refused to move. At the end of his arm, the revolver was becoming inconveniently heavy. Suddenly, he felt that it would be very difficult to turn this living man, sitting on a chair, into a truly dead one. A fleeting smile passed across Maxime Joubert's lips. The pale scar stretched out, changed shape.

'Perhaps it isn't absolutely necessary to do away with me? he said. Perhaps there's another solution, more logical, not as dirty?

Etienne wanted to scratch his elbow. The minutes he was in the process of living now formed a kind of short, self contained existence in the middle of his normal existence, a violent and risky ordeal, complete of itself, inserted into the flow of his normal days. Soon this madness was going to end, he would wake up, he would find again his familiar concerns, his bedroom, his worries, his hopes, his work. A cowardly feeling of relief took effect within him.

'In short, said Maxime Joubert, the hatred you feel towards me is motivated solely by my intention of marrying your mother. If this intention no longer existed, the idea of killing me would not occur to you?

'That's right, muttered Etienne. Give her up. disappear, if not...

With a movement of his wrist, he straightened the gun, which was pointing towards the floor.

'How shall I announce this preposterous decision to her? asked Maxime Joubert.

Now in a state of confusion, Etienne felt that his resolve was weakening and that the odds were turning in the other's favour. Disjointed ideas were running through his mind at a prodigious speed. He forced himself to think, despite the disarray which was agitating him. Then, exhausted, anxious, he whispered:

'Write a letter breaking off the relationship. Tell her that you will not be coming to dinner this evening and that you will never see her again.

Maxime Joubert smiled more broadly.

'I insist that you write this letter, yelled Etienne.

And he stepped forward.

'Alright, said Maxime Joubert. Dictate it to me.

He drew a piece of paper towards him and took a pen out of the inside pocket of his jacket. Walking around the table, Etienne came to stand to the right of the man, who continued to smile.

'I'm waiting, said Maxime Joubert.

'Why do you want me to dictate this letter?

'It corresponds so little to my feelings, that I admit that I am incapable of conceiving it myself.

Etienne leaned forward slightly. His revolver, some thirty centimetres away, was pointed at the head with its well combed grey hair. A faint aroma of tobacco and eau de Cologne penetrated his nostrils. There was no longer a single thought in his mind. He was alone. He was dying of thirst in a desert.

'Well? Maxime Joubert's voice continued.

Etienne looked up. And, suddenly, a white flash passed across his eyes. His fingers were forced violently open. He uttered a cry of pain. The revolver, torn from his hand, had fallen on the table. Maxime Joubert took the gun and slipped it into his pocket,

'There we are, he said. Now we shall be more at ease to talk.

After a moment of astonishment, blinding anger burst into Etienne's brain. His teeth were chattering. Shame, hatred were shaking his nerves. Disarmed, dispossessed, reduced to a ridiculous impotence, he repeated:

'Bastard! Bastard!...

'Why are you insulting me? said Maxime Joubert. Because I've taken your gun? Don't have me believe that your daring derived from a loaded revolver...

He was no longer smiling. His face was serious. His clear eyes expressed complete assurance.

'This letter, he continued, I promised that you would have it, and so you shall. But I don't like working under threat. Sit down and dictate.

Etienne looked at Maxime Joubert, as if to read in this face the meaning of the words he had just heard. Floored by this one reply, his rage was disappearing into the void. Why was Maxime Joubert refusing to exploit his advantage? What motive did he have in drawing up such a letter, since nothing, at the present time, was forcing him to do so. Respect for his given word? Fear of vengeance at a later date? "It doesn't matter. If I get from him the letter I want, my visit will not have been in vain. I must take advantage of the situation, before he changes his mind."

'To work, said Maxime Joubert. "My dear Marion..."

"'My dear Marion", repeated Etienne in a toneless voice.

He was finding it difficult to remain standing. Making a real effort, he continued:

"'After mature reflection, I prefer not to see you again...'"

And he thought: "In point of fact, I have used 'vous', but perhaps he uses 'tu', when he speaks to her?"

The nib scratched on the paper.

"'...not to see you again", said Maxime Joubert.

"'So do not be surprised, went on Etienne, if I do not appear for dinner this evening. And, especially, do not try to meet me in the future...'"

He hesitated for a moment. Each word he spoke was tearing at his throat. He had the impression that he was insulting Marion. As if this letter were expressing his own personal feelings, and no longer those of Maxime Joubert. As if it were he, Etienne, inflicting on his mother the humiliation of a cynical indifference.

'Carry on, said Maxime Joubert.

'Wait, murmured Etienne.

'You don't know what more to say?

'Of course I do...

He blushed and realised he was looking ridiculous, like a dunce called up to the blackboard to recite something he had not learned.

"'It is all over between us", he declared at last.

'Perfect, said Maxime Joubert. (And he wrote the sentence.) After that?

'Er...Write. write: "It's for the best. This union would have complicated your life and mine. I now understand..."

'Not so fast, please. I am at: "I now understand." Is that all?

'No. Add: "Goodbye, Marion. Forgive me..."

Etienne's voice broke. He could speak no longer. It seemed that his chest was exploding because of the violent beating of his heart.

'That's it, said Maxime Joubert. I shall sign it. I shall date it. And, as agreed, you will transmit this document to your mother.

He slipped the letter into an envelope, without sealing it, and wrote the address:

'If you would like to read it...

A hand, holding the envelope, was moving towards Etienne. But he could barely see. He had reached the limits of his unhappiness. He seemed to be floating on air through a fog of tears.

'I now have a better appreciation of your mother's concern, said Maxime Joubert. She told me that she has often regretted what she revealed to you about Louis Martin. Since that day, it seems, you have changed. You have become silent, secretive, irritable. Is that correct?

Etienne lowered his head and muttered:

'Let me go!...

'You are free to go, but I would like to say a few words...

'I won't listen to you.

'It's about Louis Martin. You have really got worked up about this business of criminal heredity. You believed that you had the makings of a murderer...

'Give me back the revolver...

'If I gave you back the revolver, you wouldn't know how to use it. In your place, Louis Martin would not have wasted his time explaining the reasons for his visit. I would have been dead even before I had been able to ask his name.

He got up, placed the letter on the corner of the table and began filling his pipe. The flame from the match sprang out and lit up the lower part of his face. A wisp of pungent smoke emerged from the bowl. Etienne took a step towards the door.

'Wait! cried Maxime Joubert. I have more to say to you...

As if dominated by a superior will, Etienne stopped. His obedience surprised even himself. He attributed it to the extreme weariness which had invaded his limbs and his brain.

'Your mother has told me that you have a passion for philosophy, continued Maxime Joubert. I, too, like philosophy.

'Good for you, said Etienne.

Maxime Joubert was drawing on his pipe, in short bursts.

'Philosophy is an admirable field of study. However, haven't you noticed that the originality of philosophers consists of setting out ancient ideas in a modern way and in finding new terms to define things as old as the earth? Engaged in this intellectual game, obsessed by the mania for systems and formulae, they become further and further removed from "life as it is lived"? One cannot explain and, consequently, constrain life as it is lived. One can only experience it in its ups and downs of joy and grief, mystery and clarity. No philosophical treatise could justify, explain, the minutes you and I are living through here and now.

Etienne shrugged his shoulders.

'You think I'm wrong? went on Maxime Joubert. You have blind confidence in a theory? Every theory is inanimate in its essence, but man brings it to life, enflames it by projecting onto it his passion. For the pleasure of proving he is right, he transforms logic into madness, manifest truth into total confusion. Do you do physical training?

Taken aback, Etienne replied:

'Yes.

'Congratulations. But when you have finished your physical training session, you do not go out into the street on all fours, on the pretext that this limbering up exercise has been recommended by your teacher. In the same way, although philosophy is considered an excellent exercise for the mind, it would be absurd to apply wholesale the principles of such or such a doctrine to every circumstance of life.

He smiled. Etienne looked away and murmured:

'What you are saying is stupid!

'Not as stupid as all that! I assure you, if philosophy is the study of life, life is not the study of philosophy. Besides, with the odd exception, philosophers have lived according to their instincts, much more than according to their reason...

Whilst speaking, he had walked towards the bookshelves. His hand slipped with familiarity across the spines of the neatly aligned volumes.

'Have you read the biographies of the philosophers you admire? he asked.

'No, said Etienne.

'That's a mistake. The story of the men is often as instructive as the exposition of their thoughts. If my memory is correct, Schopenhauer, the pessimist, who despised life and longed for oblivion, had settled in Frankfurt, because, according to the statistics, this city had a low rate of mortality. Jean-Jacques Rousseau was drawing up an exquisite theory on the education of children, whilst abandoning his own to public charity. Heidegger[11] claimed to be an apostle of individualism and of creative angst, but joined the Nazi Party for fear of police repression. And, in our own day, how many preach the delights of absurdity and manage their destiny with an infallible commercial logic?

'I know one who lives like a pariah, said Etienne defiantly.

'It will pass, sighed Maxime Joubert. Only Don Quixote[12] modelled his attitude scrupulously on the idea he had conceived of the world. You have been crammed full of philosophy. And you haven't had the time to digest it. So, don't try any more to act, to feel, according to someone else's advice. Be yourself, from your head to your toes. Just now, in front of me, you were not yourself. You were distorting your true nature. The proof is that you no longer resent me for having taken your revolver off you. Perhaps even, you no longer consider me to be wholly an enemy?..

'I hate you, pronounced Etienne in a hoarse voice.

'That's a pity. Personally, I find you rather likeable.

Once again, this hint of a smile, this honest glance, the grey of his suit and his hair, the white of his hand gripping the pipe. A rush of blood rose to Etienne's face. Turning on his heels, he made his way to the door.

'You are forgetting your letter, said Maxime Joubert.

Etienne came back, took the envelope, and, holding it in his hand, left the room without turning round. When he was in the street, a dreadful suspicion seized him. Had Maxime Joubert changed the text of the letter while he was writing? Feverishly, he unfolded the sheet of paper. On the white page, the words which he had dictated, written at speed, were all there, line by line. Etienne uttered a sigh of deliverance. "Despite everything, I've won." Fine rain, imperceptible, was falling from the sky. The asphalt was gleaming. On the pavement, people were walking, heads bowed. Etienne's watch showed twenty past seven. He took a taxi home.

The car was moving slowly. Leaning very firmly against the back of the seat, Etienne was getting his breath back and trying hard to foresee how events would unfold. After confronting Maxime Joubert, he was going to confront Marion. With her it would be easier. "Not a word about my visit to this man. I shall tell mum that I have found the envelope in our pigeonhole in the caretaker's room. Mustn't forget to seal the envelope. She will read the note, She will be shattered. And in a few days, she won't think any more about it." The driver braked. Etienne gave a start. He swore. He had forgotten the revolver. If Marion should notice that the gun had disappeared, she would immediately suspect that her son had taken it. He would have to give an explanation, invent a new lie. He was panicking, Ideas were beginning to swirl around in his head. "Keep calm. Let's consider the problem head on. It is rare for Marion to open the drawer of her bedside table. I shall write to Maxime Joubert and ask him to leave the revolver with his caretaker, or send it to me through the post. He won't refuse. He's an honourable bloke. He could have thrown me out after taking the gun off me. He will certainly have kept it. He didn't even abuse his power by humiliating me further. If it wasn't a question of Marion's future, I would perhaps enjoy seeing this man again. I must check if what he told me about Schopenhauer, Rousseau, Heidegger is correct."

The more he reflected on the circumstances of Maxime Joubert, the more he was amazed by the courage of this man, who wanted to marry Marion, despite everything he knew about her. Only a very great love, insane, overwhelming, could justify this decision to enter a milieu faithful to the memory of Louis Martin. Etienne wondered if, in Maxime Joubert's shoes, he would not have recoiled before the prospect of giving his name to a murderer's widow, to acquire the son of a murderer. And M Thuillier, so generous of spirit, so eloquent, so dogmatic, what would have been his attitude in such circumstances? And the others, the professional thinkers, the official philosophers? "But he doesn't love my mother, he doesn't love her any more. If he had loved her, he would not have agreed to write this letter. He was looking for an excuse to break off the relationship. I provided him with it. Now he is free. It is all better as it is."

His mind was becoming calmer. He stretched out his legs. At the present moment he no longer doubted that he had acted in Marion's best interests. He was imagining, for her and for himself, days of happiness stretching long into the future. Later, he would confess everything to her and she would thank him for having spared her the constraints of a hopeless marriage. "When one has been the wife of Louis Martin..." He did not complete the thought. The feeling that he was making a mistake was slipping into his mind, vague but persistent, like the start of a dizzy spell. He wanted to defend himself against this feeling of nausea and evoke, once again, the memory of his father. But, in the inner world where Etienne was summoning him to appear, Louis Martin was no longer coming. He was remaining outside, with the others. He was content to be what he had been. "I now know what the business of murder is. What I wasn't able to do, he did it, several times, deliberately. He found, within himself, at the right moment, the formidable, incredible courage to deprive a human being of his future. He dared to unravel, to sever, what had been put together by a superior will. Between the two of us there exists this difference: as brief as the moment which separates the firing of the gun from a death, as indefinable as the change in the colour of an eye which fixes itself in a stare. Nothing, almost nothing..." A slight fear pinched his chest. He lowered his head, as if to avoid the wing of a bat.

The column in the place de l'Alma disappeared, turning on itself, to let the car pass. Streets, trees, a bridge, people, the busy, absurd, chattering city, with its commerce and traffic jams. " And me, in all of this, what am I? What's going to become of me?" His mind drifted for a while on this idea, as if on a cloud. Then the taxi stopped. Etienne recognised the front of his house. Mysterious power of homes. However insane people were, they fell, at certain defined times, into the same sanctuaries. To be alive was, first of all, to live somewhere. Etienne paid the taxi driver. The rain had stopped.

'Keep the change, he said.

The driver lightly touched the peak of his cap. Safe in the porch of the house, Etienne reread the letter, stuck the envelope down and put it back in his jacket pocket.

*

An aroma of roast chicken filled the hall. Marion came out of the kitchen.

'I was worried, she said. You went off without letting me know... What time is it?

'About half past seven.

'Already? All this shopping has made me late!..

She looked at her son, curious, imploring, as if to discover what his state of mind was towards her. After the discussion they had had together in the morning, it was clear that she still hesitated to believe that he was resigned to the situation. A shadow passed across her eyes. Then she shook her head and said, in cheerful fashion:

'I've laid the table. Go and see if I've forgotten anything.

Etienne touched, with the tips of his fingers, the stiff, rectangular envelope in his pocket. It was now that he had to give it to Marion. Without allowing the time for her to prepare further, for hope to have fully taken hold. The more quickly he delivered the blow, the less she would suffer from the wound. All the while repeating that, in the present circumstances, it would be kinder to be ruthless, he crossed the threshold of the dining room and stopped still, dazzled. The lamps of the chandelier were lit. An old flowered shawl (taken from which cupboard?) entirely hid the sewing machine from view. The rolls of material, the patterns, the scissors had disappeared. The table was covered with a cloth with starched pleats. In the centre of this field of snow, camellia blooms lay in water in a flat crystal receptacle. All around in rows, lay dishes laden with hors d'oeuvre. A bottle of red wine stood guard over this appetising spread. The table was laid for three people. Serviettes, in wallet folds, lay in white plates patterned with streaks of blue.

'It will be a very simple little meal, said Marion.

She had come in behind him to seek his approval. With a lump in his throat, he murmured:

'Yes, mum...

Better than anything which might have been confided to him, the sight of this table, decorated and laid with care, bore witness to the importance which his mother attached to the visit of Maxime Joubert. The marinated anchovies and mushrooms à la grecque spoke volumes about the one who had bought them. The olives and foie gras en gelée became proofs of love. Could it be that so much expense and so much preparation should utterly go to waste? He turned towards Marion. She was smiling anxiously, bravely, her face made up. A black suit, brought in at the waist, lent to her outline a little element of simplicity and seriousness in this decor of light.

'You've gone to a lot of trouble, Marion, he said in a muted tone.

'Not at all. If you knew how much pleasure it has given me to arrange everything!..

He thought that she must have taken into account Maxime Joubert's preferences in putting together the menu and choosing the wines. This notion was the final straw for his feeling of confusion. Again his trembling fingers felt the envelope deep in his pocket. The letter was a weapon, even more to be dreaded than the revolver. Once more he had, within reach of his hand, the wherewithal to destroy a life. The victim was there, unaware of the danger, happy to be a woman, certain of giving pleasure. "And yet, I must act. I have gone too far. I cannot go back." He took the letter, between thumb and forefinger, extracted it slowly from its hiding place.

'I'm going back into the kitchen, said Marion. I must keep an eye on the chicken.

He pushed the envelope back in his pocket. This delay, which he had not sought, seemed to him to be beneficial. In front of the table, laid and prepared, he was recovering his strength and trying to think calmly. He recalled Maxime Joubert's words: "Life as it is lived...one cannot explain it...one can only experience it, in its ups and downs of joy and grief, mystery and clarity..." Marion had jumped up to her neck into this life as it is lived; the tablecloth, the chicken, the electric lights were the indisputable symbols. She was drawing her pleasure from the humblest of springs. Whereas he... The peppery aroma of the hors-d'oeuvre was delicately tickling his nostrils. With astonishment, with indignation, he realised that he was hungry. At a moment such as this? It was almost indecent. All his mind was rebelling against the irritating demands of his stomach. He took a step back and leaned against the wall. He felt physically sick. "He will not come. We shall have to sit down at table opposite each other. Eat all this, the two of us. And Marion will be so sad! How will I console her? The foie gras, the tomato slices...It's impossible... impossible...His eyes took in the tablecloth, the place settings, the dishes, as if they were an impregnable fortress. He felt defeated simply by the presence of the flowers and the food. He capitulated before the everyday necessities of life.

Marion's voice rang out:

'Cut the bread, Etienne.

'Yes, mum.

'Thin slices...

He took the bread from the sideboard and chose a well sharpened knife. The blade was cutting into the crust with a pleasant cracking sound. Crumbs were falling on the tablecloth. Gradually, the idea that Maxime Joubert could come into this room, sit down, eat, talk, smile in front of Marion, no longer seemed unacceptable. He could even imagine him very well, sitting in this familiar decor, with his grey hair, his bright eyes and his little scar. Truth to tell, he almost wanted to see him again, to hear him again. "What's the matter with me? I hate him and I want him to come. But it's for her, only for her."

He placed the pieces of bread in the wicker basket:

'I've done it, mum.

'The white wine is behind the window, in a bowl with ice. It's going to be too cold. Perhaps you ought to open it…

It was a tall, delicate bottle, with a yellow cap: Traminer. Etienne opened the drawer of the sideboard, grasped a corkscrew and gripped the bottle between his legs. There was a clanging of saucepans. He felt as if he were being hoodwinked by a mean-minded devil. A dreadful sinking feeling was overtaking him. As if his soul had turned in on itself, in his head. He remembered the words of the letter: "It is all over between us… this union would have complicated your life and mine."

Each word, intended to wound Marion, was wounding himself. He was discovering that he was responsible for a catastrophe beyond measure. Everything in his behaviour, until that moment, seemed to be the work of a madman. The cork popped as it came out. Etienne put the bottle on the table. And Marion suspecting nothing! A wave of uncontrollable pity propelled him toward this woman, his mother, who was busy in the kitchen and dreaming of happiness as she poured the piping hot sauce over the chicken. To know her so humble, so courageous, before the mystery of the future, rendered her doubly loveable to him. He could not bear the thought of disappointing her. The violence of his conviction was such that tears filled his eyes. "What to do? How to repair the damage?" It was like an outpouring, from his shattered body, of a thousand drops of water and blood. With a furious gesture, he thrust his hand into his pocket and crumpled the letter. At all costs, Maxime Joubert had to come to dinner this evening. "Telephone him. Not from here, of course. There's a telephone kiosk in the café next door. I'll go. I'll speak to him. He'll think I'm mad. I don't care. Perhaps he will refuse? No, he won't be able to. I shall convince him…" Like someone deranged, he rushed into the hall.

'Where are you going, Etienne? asked Marion.

He paused for a moment, got his breath back and replied weakly:

'To buy some cigarettes, mum.

'Don't be too long, my darling.

On the staircase he hurtled down the steps, two by two, without holding onto the banister rail. This jerky motion responded to a need within him for physical exertion. Out of breath, his mouth open, he ran past the caretaker's room, went out into the street, rushed into the restaurant with its wide, brightly lit windows. By a stroke of luck the telephone kiosk was free. Rapidly, he leafed through the directory, which had been left on a shelf. The stained, crumpled pages were barely visible: Élysées 92-50. Etienne dialled the number and waited, his stomach tense, his ears buzzing. The regular ringing bored into his eardrum. A click rang out. At the other end of the line, the voice of the housekeeper asked:

'Hello? How may I help?

Etienne pressed the telephone button and the token dropped into the box with a hollow noise.

'I would like to speak to M. Maxime Joubert, he said.

'I shall go and see if Monsieur is still here. Who is speaking, please?

'It's M. Etienne Martin.

The housekeeper went off and was replaced by a large black void. Etienne bit his lip. He had foreseen everything, except the fact that Maxime Joubert, after handing him the letter, had been able to make something of his evening by dining in town with friends. If that was the situation, how would Etienne dare confront his mother? Would he let her wait indefinitely for her guest to arrive. Or would he admit to her, in all honesty, the abominable scheming which explained this absence? A fit of panic gripped his mind at the very prospect of such a painful confession.

"Oh God, let him still be there! Make him come to the 'phone! Let him hear me, let him save me!" His ear, stuck to the receiver, was getting hot, seemed to be swelling. A trickle of sweat ran down his right cheek. Suddenly he gave a start, as pure joy struck him like a thunderbolt. Maxime Joubert's voice:

'Hello, Etienne?

He closed his eyes and stammered:

'Yes.

'What's happening?

'I didn't give her the letter...I couldn't...

There was a silence. Etienne, overwhelmed, worn out, opened his eyes. The walls of the kiosk were marked with various inscriptions, telephone numbers, hearts pierced with arrows, girls' Christian names.

'You did the right thing, Maxime Joubert said at last. I admit that I have been impatient to hear from you...

'You knew that I would telephone?

'Do you believe that I would have given you that letter, if I had supposed, for one second, that you would have carried out your plan?

Etienne jumped:

'So you were making fun of me?

'No. I gave you the opportunity to accept your responsibilities, towards your mother and towards myself. I trusted you. Are you going to blame me for that?

Etienne did not reply. After what he had lived through, all rebellion seemed impossible.

'Where are you speaking from? continued Maxime Joubert.

'From a restaurant, said Etienne.

He hesitated a moment and said in a gloomy voice:

'I'm sorry. Mum doesn't know anything about it. She's waiting for you. You must come.

It seemed that his life was draining from him with these last words. As Maxime Joubert was not saying anything, he murmured again in a beseeching tone:

'Come, please, it's vital.

'I'm coming, said Maxime Joubert.

And he hung up.

Etienne came out of the kiosk and crossed the room stiffly, like a sleepwalker. In the mirror above the counter, he noticed a tall young man, thin and blond, haggard, unkempt, gliding through the bluish cigarette smoke. The lukewarm air of the street caressed his face. He sat down on a bench under a lamppost. A sad weariness was gradually creeping over him, in the way that darkness takes hold of the sky. With his nerves at breaking point, he opened himself to this mellow sensation of defeat and deliverance. In the very depths of his being he felt that he had asked more of life than life could give. Yes, that was it: the one who wishes to crush the order of the universe is met with the resistance offered by words, objects and the souls of men. He had been ignorant of this. He had believed himself to be a philosopher among philosophers, and his ignorance had almost ended in disaster. Now, having avoided the worst, he was turning away from his delusions and hoping for no more from life than a little peace and quiet for his studies, for friendship and tenderness. The essential thing, at the end of this struggle, was that Marion should be happy. "All for her." A long time passed, during which he dreamed of his future. The movement and the noise of the avenue washed around him, as if he were a solitary reef.

Suddenly he stood up. A car, black and low to the ground, had just parked, twenty metres from him, against the pavement. Maxime Joubert got out, closed the door and disappeared into the porch of the block of flats. Etienne's lips exhaled a muffled groan. A bus rumbled by, uncomplicated, with its row of faces seemingly mounted under glass. "He's getting out of the lift. He's ringing at the door. She's opening it. She's falling into his arms." A moment more, and Etienne looked at the fronts of the buildings, the sky, the cars driving along the avenue de Tourville. Then, step by step, unhurried, he made his way, in his turn, towards the house. On the landing, he experienced, one last time, the desire to escape, to flee. A manly voice penetrated the solid wood door. Etienne was no longer in his own home. He was visiting his mother. Forgetting that he had a key in his pocket, he pushed the button of the door bell. The door opened. The lights were shining. The furniture and the walls had taken on a new appearance. A man's hat was hanging on the coat stand. The very air was not the same as usual.

As if under the influence of a dream, Etienne saw Marion, who was coming towards him, light on her feet, anxious, unrecognisable. Her face seemed carved from a translucent material, from which the signs of tiredness and wear had disappeared.

There was a gently questioning look in her eyes. She took her son's arm and led him into the dining room. The man was there, standing in front of the table. A hand reached out towards Etienne. He grasped it without thinking, with the feeling of being rescued from a shipwreck. His heart was filled with an unexpected joy. Marion said:

'May I introduce you: my son, M Maxime Joubert.

NOTES

Chapter One

1 Jean-Jacques Rousseau (1712 – 1778), born in Geneva, was a philosopher who believed in the innate goodness of mankind. He was an early proponent of human rights and a key figure in the Enlightenment.

2 Arthur Schopenhauer (1788 – 1860) was a German philosopher. An atheist, he is associated with Existentialism (see note on Chapter Eight).

Chapter Two

1 Victor Hugo (1802 – 1885) was a poet, novelist, and dramatist of the Romantic school. He entered politics later in life.

2 Stendhal (1783 – 1842) was a novelist and travel writer. Stendhal was a pen name.

3 Alphonse de Lamartine (1790 – 1869) was a poet of the Romantic school. He too entered French politics and rose to the position of Foreign Secretary in 1848.

Chapter Six

1 Eudemonism is an ethical doctrine holding that the value of moral action lies in its capacity to produce happiness.

2 St. Thomas Aquinas (1225 – 1274) was born in what is now central Italy. He was a Dominican friar, Catholic priest, philosopher and theologian. He was highly influential in Western thought.

3 Plato (?427 – ?348 BC) was a Greek philosopher. He is considered to be the pivotal figure in Western philosophy.

4 Immanuel Kant (1724 – 1804) was a German philosopher and another key figure in the Enlightenment.

5 Herbert Spencer (1820 – 1903) was an English philosopher and evolutionary biologist.

6 Jean-Marie Guyau (1854 – 1888) was a French philosopher and poet.

7 Henri-Louis Bergson (1859 – 1941) was a French philosopher, who was very influential in the first half of the twentieth century.

Chapter Eight

1 Here M Thuillier is expounding elements of the system of philosophical thought known as Existentialism. The first existentialist is usually considered to be Kirkegaard (see note below), although he never used the term. His branch of Existentialism was the Christian one. M Thuillier makes a brief, disdainful reference to this in Chapter Nine on page 95. In Chapter Eight we encounter the atheistic branch, which was very much in vogue in certain French intellectual circles in the mid twentieth century.

Its best known proponent was Jean-Paul Sartre (1905 – 1980). At the time of the publication of *La Tête sur les Epaules* (1951), Sartre would have been a familiar name to readers of the book, by virtue of his novels, plays and Marxist political activism. Most readers would also have had some idea, however vague, of what Existentialism was about.

This is not the place for a detailed account of Existentialism (and I am not the person to undertake it!), but suffice it to say that many have found aspects of Existentialism unacceptably bleak, from the point of view both of the individual and of society.

What Troyat gives us here is a satire of Existentialism. See, for example, the pretentious and meaningless phrases in italics (on page 78). Moreover, M Thuillier bears a striking physical resemblance to Sartre, even in the glasses he wears. Thus it is safe to assume that Troyat is satirising not only Sartre's philosophy, but the man himself.

A crucial element in the novel is the contrast between M Thuiller's attitude towards philosophy and Maxine Joubert's, as expressed in Chapter Ten, pages 134 – 136. See also the brief discussion on the subject between Marion and Etienne in Chapter Nine, pages 89 and 90.

2 Soren Kirkegaard (1813 – 1855), born in Copenhagen, was a Christian philosopher, theologian, author and poet.

3 Karl Jaspers (1883 – 1969) was a German psychiatrist and philosopher.

Chapter Nine

1 vélo-solex – a small, economical type of moped, very popular with students of the time.

Chapter Ten

1 Tiberius, Nero and Caligula were Roman emperors infamous for their cruelty and brutality. The Borgias, a family of immense wealth and power in the Europe of the fifteenth and sixteenth centuries, had a similar reputation.

2 Francois-René Chateaubriand (1768 – 1848) was a French author, politician, diplomat and historian. He was a writer of the Romantic school.

3 Alphonse Daudet (1840 – 1897) was a French novelist

4 Anatole France (1844 – 1924) was a French poet, novelist and journalist, who enjoyed considerable popularity in his lifetime.

5 Charles Baudelaire (1821 – 1867) was a French poet, whose work has remained popular.

6 Arthur Rimbaud (1854 – 1891) was a French poet. Again, his work is still highly regarded.

7 Students of French of my era will recall that some texts were bound with their pages folded; they had to be carefully cut open!

8 Baruch Spinoza (1632 – 1677), born in Amsterdam, was one of the early philosophers of the Enlightenment. He was also a forerunner of modern biblical study.

9 Sigmund Freud (1856 – 1939) was an Austrian psychologist and the founder of psychoanalysis.

10 Gottfried Leibniz (1646 – 1716) was a German philosopher, mathematician, scientist and diplomat – a true polymath, indeed.

11 Martin Heidegger (1889 – 1976), born in Messkirch, Germany, is widely regarded as one of the most influential of philosophers of the twentieth century.

12 Don Quixote. There is, of course, a profound irony here, in that Don Quixote is a purely fictitious character, created in the novel of the same name by the Spanish author, Miguel de Cervantes (1547 – 1616).